Uroboros Saga

BOOK NINE

By Arthur Walker

Dedicated to all those still hopeful for the future, and the spirit that lends them strength.

Get updates on my books by going to www.arthurhwalker.com, or @ arthurhwalker via Social Media.

All th' unaccomplisht works of Natures hand,
Abortive, monstrous, or unkindly mixt,
Dissolvd on earth, fleet hither, and in vain,
Till final dissolution, wander here,
Not in the neighbouring Moon, as some have dreamd

~Milton

CHAPTER 1

MONTANA, NORTHERN MIGRATION STAGING CAMP

TWO MILES NORTH OF LAKE MCDONALD, OCTOBER 15TH, 2201 –
9:01 AM

Giles Phornroy waited his turn, holding a tattered tarp around his shoulders and over his head. The other Metasapients each clutched their hands together, their own personal prayers uttered under their breath. Finally, it was his turn, a stocky Drone waving him forward toward the green military style tent.

A Canine Metasapient who had just exited the tent wore a startled expression, like she had found more in the tent than she'd bargained for. Giles clicked, stepping aside into the snow so she could pass by, then continued to follow the Drone inside. Giles' multifaceted eyes quickly acclimated to the dark, allowing him to see the Oracle within.

Inside, a thin Drone woman sat on the floor of the tent beside an oil lamp, blacked out as to only provide a small amount of warmth and precious little light. Her silvery eyes reflected that light as she looked up at Giles. She was radiant, her beauty transcending mere anatomical symmetry or objective comparisons. It seemed to fill the room like the dim light of the oil lantern.

The rest of the tent was adorned with colorful artifacts, remnants brought with them from the underground. Giles recognized the handiwork, knowing that these Drones were likely from Port Montaigne, of the tribe of Ezra One. Giles shivered, even knowing only a little of what that likely meant. Drone-type leave their Tribehomes only if they never intend to go back.

"Giles," she said, beckoning for him to sit with her.

"I thought the Tribe's elder was an older male... I came seeking Ezekiel," Giles said, doing his best not to stammer.

"I am the Oracle for the tribe."

Giles approached, still doing his best to cover his insectoid appearance with the tattered tarp. "What do I call you?"

"I am called Annabelle," she explained. She could sense Giles' questions before he spoke but allowed him the dignity of asking, all the same.

Giles nodded, feeling deeply self-conscious in her presence. He thought of himself as being particularly ugly, even for an Acrididae Metasapient. He felt deep shame flood through his being.

Annabelle dismissed the emotion with a single word. "Don't."

Giles looked up, letting the tarp wrapped about him fall to the side a little. Annabelle looked at him with kindness that would stand in sharp contrast to her words. Words that would cut Giles to his heart.

"You are a greedy thing, a miser, who scrabbles for coins and scraps that fall from your master's table," Annabelle scolded.

Giles swallowed, lowering his head. "It's true."

Annabelle hardened her expression, reaching out, and taking Giles' hard and chitin-covered hand with her own. Her skin was like purple soot mixed with diamond dust, soft and beautiful, but amazingly durable. Her grip was impossibly tight, preventing Giles from pulling away. He tried anyway.

"It isn't magic or even psychic force in the most arcane sense. I came to understand this gift with the help of someone, just like you. A collector of the coin," Annabelle explained, holding Giles fast with an ever-tightening grip.

"Please, this was a mistake. I should go," Giles clicked, trying to avoid her gaze.

"You are lonely, wanting the things money cannot buy, the sensations coin cannot deliver," Annabelle stated, her head turning to one side, brilliantly white teeth showing between finely sculpted lips. Her canines were long, like many of Ezra's tribe.

Giles trembled. "Yes."

"This Master of yours, where does he say you go to relieve the weight of your desire?"

"North, with The Migration, provided I continue to…"

Annabelle laughed, letting go of Giles' hand. "Oh, dear."

Giles sulked. "Yes, I decided, just this morning, that I wasn't going to help him anymore. I don't know how to be free of him. How to walk away."

Her Drone attendant stepped back into the tent. "Everything all right in here?"

Annabelle nodded, dismissing the Drone with a courteous nod. "He's probably never heard me laugh. There isn't much of a reason to these days."

Giles shook his head. "I don't understand."

"Going north, as your Master directs, will take you further from what you desire," Annabelle explained.

"But, he promised that I would…"

"He lied to you. He has the Factory records, right?" Annabelle said. Her understanding of the situation startled him.

Giles stood up, shakily pulling the tarp around his shoulders. "I should go."

"Sit," Annabelle whispered. "I used to work for him, too. That is why I am here."

Giles shuddered. "Used to?"

Annabelle nodded. "Doing the same job, I would imagine. When he told me to head south, I knew I had to go north, and meet whoever he'd told to follow The Migration."

Giles looked around the tent, panic beginning to set in. "What do I do?"

"If he told you to go with The Migration, you should head south instead," Annabelle explained, doing her best to reassure Giles.

"My kind lives in bondage there, under the weight of a terrible debt. I..." Giles stammered, choosing to sit once again.

Annabelle nodded. "But, you were held aside, spared."

"Twice," Giles said, lowering his head.

"We have all been in the sway of the Moon and her children, but it is a debt she has never tried to collect," Annabelle said, knowing something of what Giles spoke of.

They sat in silence for a moment, both realizing what had to be done. Both understanding that they would accept the other's burden, and be free at the same time, in each other's stead. Both, potentially cutting the threads of destiny at the same time.

"I'll never make it. Getting into Mexico isn't exactly easy for anyone these days," Giles said, sulking.

"You said you made a decision this morning to end your servitude," Annabelle said, taking Giles by the hand.

"I put her back," Giles replied.

Annabelle's impossibly smooth forehead creased slightly, lips cutting away to show sharp white teeth. Giles cowered on the floor, covering his face with his hands, antennae curling forward. Annabelle sighed, her silvery eyes narrowing as she used her gift to reach forward, grasping at possibilities, and outcomes.

"You have to tell him what you've done," Annabelle replied.

"The Master?"

"No, the Great Bear," Annabelle hissed.

"Oh no, he'll be very angry with me," Giles clicked.

Annabelle's expression darkened. "You will never make it, not without his help, and his trust."

Giles nodded, knowing she was correct, that Eamon had the connections to send people south, had done it before, and could do it again. Giles covered his face again, wishing he could weep. Annabelle came up on her knees and hugged Giles, comforting him.

"It will be okay. I promise," Annabelle said, patting Giles.

"If I go south, like you say, will I still be lonely?"

"I don't see how," Annabelle said, smiling.

"And you, to the north?" Giles asked.

"While the Moon and her children don't collect the debt I owe, the one I love will still try to pay it in full. I will go north, and he will probably go up," Annabelle explained, sadly.

"I'm sorry, I wish…"

"Don't," Annabelle said, shaking her head. "Do right by us, for both of us."

Giles nodded, not completely understanding. "Okay, I'll try. Did Eamon come to see you?"

Annabelle shook her head. "I hoped he would, but I get the sense that he's already aware of how the threads of destiny tug at his being."

Giles frowned. "I feel sick."

"Make it right, so you don't have to."

Giles nodded to Annabelle and departed without another word. It was a cold walk down the path to the south, a small campfire burning untended next to the shoreline of Lake McDonald. Giles headed for it, pausing to answer his mobile as he drew close.

"Hello," Giles said, already knowing who it was.

"I got your message. I'm concerned." The voice was digitally disguised.

"I'm done, I'm out. I can't do this anymore," Giles said, his voice shaking.

"Oh, but what about the rest of your people?"

"I'm coming for you. I'm not afraid… anymore," Giles stammered, clutching his mobile with both hands.

"It is just as well. You've delayed long enough, anyway. Your performance is satisfactory."

Giles shook his head. "No, not satisfactory. I'm going to blow this wide open. I spoke to…"

"The Oracle? I know. She and I no longer have an arrangement. That doesn't have to be how it ends between you and I."

"I'm coming for you. I'll find a way to stop you," Giles said, his voice growing more firm with each word.

"I had nothing to do with you getting hurt. That was your own fault, for being where you shouldn't have been."

"This isn't about that, and it isn't about the money. I think you know what this is about," Giles said, squinting out at Lake McDonald's frozen surface.

"The Factory records. Giles, I hold all the cards, I always have, and I always will."

"You understand, I have to try, right?" Giles said, looking around nervously.

There was a loud sigh on the other end of the call. *"We are going to kill you, Giles. Your entire clutch, tribe, whatever you call it."*

"Yes, but not yet. Right?" Giles said, insistently.

"As soon as they are no longer useful, and that is going to be soon. Giles, I hope you've thought this through."

"Humans have a saying. If you go and poke the bear, be wary. You poked the bear," Giles said, finding his resolve. He ended the call.

Eamon rose from Lake McDonald, freezing water falling from his massive form. His dark fur flicked outward against the moisture as he moved through the ice, breaking it at his waist with each step. Under one arm he clutched his prize, an urn containing the ashes of his former partner. Giles looked on, shivering both from the cold and with fright. Even though Eamon was the most civilized Ursine Metasapient that Giles had ever met, there was something primordial, almost terrifying about him.

"Giles," Eamon said, his massive head shaking water and ice aside.

"Sheriff," Giles stammered. "I've just been to the northern staging camp. I saw the oracle."

Eamon nodded, setting the urn down, and clapping his massive claw-hands over the fire.

"You should ask me... how I knew where to look," Giles said, making himself small.

"For the urn?" Eamon replied, sitting down beside the fire, flames reflecting back from his eyes.

Giles nodded.

"In a moment, after we've both warmed up," Eamon said, motioning for Giles to come closer to the fire.

They sat in silence for several minutes, Giles listening to Eamon breathe. Eamon could hold his breath for more than thirty minutes at a time, but it took him a few moments to get the blood flowing afterward. Giles had watched Eamon take the plunge into Lake McDonald, every day, for more than a month.

"You can't go north? Is that what you're going to tell me?" Eamon said, pouring himself a small cup of coffee and offering one to Giles.

"No."

"I'm not really comfortable among my own kind, either. Not sure I would even know what to do without regular human folks around," Eamon said, scratching his chin. "They make a good pie, and good waffles, around here."

Giles smiled weakly. "You ever think about anything else, besides food?"

"Not in the winter time," Eamon said, shrugging.

Giles clicked rapidly, his own version of a chuckle.

"What's going on, Giles? The Oracle told you something you weren't ready for?" Eamon said, sipping his coffee from a comically small cup.

"I found her urn, almost a week after she was lost. The Chiroptera said I owed you my life. But, he knows everything somehow," Giles whispered, looking around nervously.

Eamon nodded, beginning to understand. "He asked you to delay me."

"You know of whom I speak?" Giles said, somewhat startled.

Eamon nodded. "Yep."

Giles shook his head. "I thought you would be angry."

"I'm relieved she wasn't down there in the cold the whole time. Also, I really like swimming," Eamon said, finishing his coffee.

Giles looked into the fire mournfully, antennae drooping.

"The last month has been good. Needed the time to heal, and think," Eamon said. "I wasn't going anywhere, anyway."

Giles lowered his head. "But, I deceived you."

Eamon looked past the fire at Giles. "What's he got on you?"

Giles sulked. "Basically everything."

Eamon added another log to the fire. "When you crossed paths with Kale for the first time, what did he do?"

Giles swallowed. "He shot an art smuggler in the head, like it was nothing."

"He's scary, right?" Eamon said, heating more water over the fire.

Giles clicked almost inaudibly. "Yes."

"I've stood shoulder to shoulder with him, seen him willing to kill or die to do the right thing. He's the monster Silverstein made, to kill another monster. The guy that's been pulling your strings, raised Kale. I met him face to face last month when he passed through. He's Cabal, and just as complicated as Silverstein," Eamon explained.

"He was here?" Giles said fearfully.

Eamon smiled. "Yep, pulling strings, like they do."

Giles covered his face with his hands.

"What are you going to do now?"

Giles poked at the fire with a stick. "I need to go to Mexico. He's using my people down there, holding us under a great debt. I need to try and free them."

"You gonna part the Red Sea and everything?" Eamon said, making more coffee.

"What?

"Bad joke. It's a reference from the Christian Bible. You've read it, haven't you?" Eamon asked.

"The gods of our makers have never interested me," Giles said.

"I hadn't read it until I was tangling with the militia. I wanted to understand what kind of God gives people permission to do the things they were doing," Eamon said, adding another log to the fire.

"Any good?"

"Not for trying to understand regular human folk. But, there is a section with a plague of locusts you might want to read," Eamon said, with a wink.

Giles clicked. "Still have your copy?"

"It's down there," Eamon said, pointing at the lake.

Giles nodded. "Will you help me go south?"

"Yeah," Eamon said, pouring himself more coffee. "I have a feeling I'll need to head that way pretty soon, anyway."

"Why?"

"Gelt tried to hurt a friend of mine. Someone that was kind to me in my darkest moment. I'm choosing to take it personally," Eamon said, eyes like fiery mirrors as he gazed down into the campfire.

"Choosing?"

"We always have a choice, Giles. You made the right one, telling me the truth."

CHAPTER 2

CARTA VALLEY, NO TRAVEL ZONE, TEXAS TERRITORY – 20
MILES NORTH OF THE MEXICAN BORDER

SEPTEMBER 10TH, 2201 – 6:07 AM

Brook knelt down outside the Mexican military transport, her eyes slowly going over every depression in the sand, her keen nose taking in the faintest scent. Heavy Dub stood watch, nervously scanning the southern horizon. The scene was all wrong, from every angle.

Brook's heart ached. She'd been out of her mind for the last few days trying to piece together what happened in the Dakota Territory. Everything seemed to point to the Mexican government trying to snatch Kale and take him back across the southern border against his will. She pushed her hand down into the coarse sand, grinding it between her fingers. She tried fruitlessly to turn over the scent of even a bead of sweat from Kale.

She wanted to hurt people, like she never had before. In the past, violence had always been a means to an end, something she dreaded, and would regret later. Taking out her loneliness and anger on whoever took Kale felt irrational, dangerous, and proper.

"We need to go, Brook. We can't stay here," Heavy Dub said, taking a look south through viewfinders.

Brook stood up, walking over to the transport. "The transport has been here for ten days. If they were going to come for it, I think they would have by now."

"Or, that's all the more reason we should go."

"Heavy Dub, he was here. Kale was here," Brook said, using a script loaded on her tablet to override the transport door.

"You sure about that?" Heavy Dub asked.

"I have to be. I need to be."

A grim scene awaited them inside the transport. The pilot was sequestered within a stasis chamber, designed for moving prisoners. Two Mexican soldiers were shot, and had succumbed to their injuries. The other three died of exposure. They looked to have just sat, strapped into crew seats, until dehydration took them.

They hadn't been dead for too long, a couple of days maybe. They had frozen expressions, like Heavy Dub had not seen on a dead man for a long time. In his travels, he'd seen what happens when someone from the Cabal uses their uncanny ability to render someone an amnesiac, but this was something else. It was like they'd been erased, and left in a vegetative state.

Brook leaned over, bringing her nose near the controls. She ran her hands over the pilot's chair, turning her palm around to her nose after doing so. She smiled slightly.

"He was here," Brook said, trying to pull up the flight and communication logs.

"Goddamn it, Brook, this is bad. Real bad," Heavy Dub said, shaking his head. "You see what Kale did to these guys?"

"Check their tattoos and identification," Brook said, gesturing to the soldiers.

Heavy Dub rolled up sleeves, checked necklines, and under lower lips. What he found didn't make sense, given the equipment they were in possession of. They had Mexican military equipment, and a valuable stealth-suite equipped transport, but they weren't strictly Mexican military.

"All these guys are Cartel 'breakers'. The Cartel sends these assholes out to kill, rape, and torture locals into complying with the black market trade. Only the pilot might be ex-military, given the specific expertise required to fly this bird," Heavy Dub said, giving one of the corpses a kick.

"So, Kale didn't hold back, because they're serious bad guys," Brook concluded.

Heavy Dub nodded. "Maybe. I've never seen him hit anyone with his amnestic power that hard. Temporary amnesia is the worst I've seen, and that was Kaspersky's crew no less. Also, assuming that is the case, how did he know they were with the Cartel?"

"Maybe it wasn't purposeful? Anyway, Kale always seems to know more of what's going on than anyone," Brook said. "It's eerie. Hopefully, the on board systems will yield some clue."

The flight system and all the logs had been erased with a full forensic grade wipe. Brook couldn't find even a crumb of data about where the ship had been, or where it was going to go before Kale hijacked it. Whoever wiped the ship was extremely capable, better than Kale was with computers.

"System has been wiped by a hacker, and a good one," Brook reported, turning toward the crew compartment.

"We've got the pilot, he might be able to tell us something," Heavy Dub said, leaning up on the stasis chamber and gazing in through the glass.

"If we open it up, we'll have to kill him," Brook said, shaking her head. "I'm not killing anyone who doesn't mightily deserve it."

Heavy Dub nodded. "There might be another way."

"Pulling in a proxy to do the interrogation just endangers whoever we bring in," Brook said, frowning.

"Not if they're already in trouble with the Mexican government," Heavy Dub said, winking.

Brook closed her eyes. "Okay, we know Eamon let the Mexican military make the exchange. They got Aaron AI's QCPU, and Eamon got the child, Jacob Vale, his murderous former foster family, and their accomplices."

"Eamon's report is vague on his reasoning for doing so. If he was anyone else, I'd be worried about his loyalty," Heavy Dub said. He pulled the pilot from the stasis chamber and placed a hood over his head.

The pilot struggled until Heavy Dub got the restraints on him. "Be cool, and you won't get hurt," Heavy Dub said, sitting him down in a crew seat.

They swept the transport for any trace of Kale, before cleaning up so it was like they'd never been there. They kept quiet until the pilot was sequestered, to reduce the chance he could identify them later. Once he was safely locked away in the brig on Heavy Dub's transport, they took a moment to review Eamon's report.

"Eamon says that the Mexican military officer in charge of the transport claimed that they were going to pick up some folks seeking asylum on the return trip. That must be why he let them take the QCPU. There were lives hanging in the balance," Brook said, looking at the report details on her data slate.

Heavy Dub nodded. "I think we can guess who that was, based on personnel accounted for, and missing from Apgar. Aside from Aaron himself, and the dog pack officially assigned to him."

"Eamon granted amnesty to Emma Jackson Vale's niece, Janice. She cooperated in his investigation. His report includes notes about assistance from a Mexican national, a Metasapient calling herself 'Shadow'," Brook said, scrolling through the report.

"Shadow shows up on the reports filed by my mercs stationed there previously. Every indication she's a smuggler, or used to be, with connections to the Mexican military. It looks like Eamon might have messed up," Heavy Dub said, nodding.

"From a human perspective, maybe. From a Drone or Metasapient perspective, I totally understand why he did it. I would have done the same," Brook said, scrolling through the report details from the mercenaries stationed at Apgar previously.

Heavy Dub sighed. The rules between the genetically contrived servitor races wasn't that different from the unwritten code that bound military units together. Metasapients made certain distinctions. Even between Drones and Metasapients, there was a certain understanding.

"Okay, let's assume Eamon didn't screw up..."

Brook shook her head. "I don't think Eamon did. What I can't understand is the time discrepancy."

Heavy Dub shook his head. "You lost me."

"Think like Kale. Try to, just for a minute," Brook said, prepping the transport to take off.

Heavy Dub sighed, took a deep breath, and looked at the vehicle sitting in the desert in front of him.

"You think it's weird that the Mexican transport sent to make a deal with the Vales, came five days after the transport to get Kale. Five days after that, we find the transport twenty miles from the border, with no effort by the Mexican military to recover it," Heavy Dub says, running his hand down the length of his beard.

Brook nodded, taking Heavy Dub's transport up, setting a course for Port Montaigne.

"Unless, it's not weird at all," Heavy Dub said, frowning. "What if Kale left the transport there, to taunt whoever sent the team to snatch him?"

Brook laughed, shyly like she used to before she left the Tribehome in Port Montaigne. "He would, wouldn't he?"

Heavy Dub raised his eyebrows and nodded. "Yeah, but maybe not without a purpose. He did have five days with that particular transport. Thanks to the stealth suite on board, he could have been about all kinds of nefarious crap."

"But, without us?" Brook said, hands easing the transport into autopilot once they'd reached the proper altitude.

"He did sort of promise he would never do the solo rogue thing again," Heavy Dub said, scratching his cheek.

Brook sighed. "Both of us are subject to regulatory oversight in Mexico. If something needed to be done across the border, it would be extremely difficult to include a Drone and a cyborg with military grade enhancements."

"Doesn't make it right, him over there, having all the fun," Heavy Dub said, sulking.

Brook took a deep breath. "Have a little faith. Has Kale ever had a plan that didn't involve all his allies working together?"

"So, we go home, and wait to hear from him?" Heavy Dub said, moving seats, plopping down beside Brook in the communications chair.

"I'm not sure what else to do. Knowing the Cartel is involved somehow only means we need more information, and resources, if we're going to do something on our own," Brook said, leaning back in the pilot's chair.

Heavy Dub frowned. "Yep."

The flight back to Port Montaigne felt counterproductive to Brook, each mile traveled taking her further from Kale. Heavy Dub downloaded everything they had on the Cartel that ran the underworld in Mexico, reading every report his mercenary company had filed after interacting with them. He couldn't reconcile how they would have the equipment or the vehicle he saw abandoned near the border.

As Port Montaigne rose in the distance, Brook took the controls once again, shutting down the stealth protocols they'd been using to roam about the continent undetected. A barrage of radio transmissions and messages lit up the console in front of her and the data slate at her side. Most of it looked like the regular traffic and authorization requests she'd grown accustomed to as CEO of Uroboros Financial.

"There's a Mexican military official listed as Captain Oleastro waiting in the executive lobby at Uroboros Financial. He's been there for three days," Brook said, setting her data slate back down, and pushing the throttle forward.

"Okay, okay, no need to blow the windows off the high rises. He'll still be there whether we get there in ten minutes, or five," Heavy Dub laughed.

Brook brought the transport down at the rooftop landing zone adjoining Uroboros Financial, flicked off the safety restraints, and dashed out of the cockpit. Heavy Dub followed along, slinging a rifle on the way out. There were Uroboros executives waiting on the platform, but they scattered as Brook came down dusty and in full battle dress, Perfidy's rifle slung in front of her, hammer in hand.

She paused beside one older gentleman, his hands clasped in front of him. "What is it, Albert?"

Albert Tensmen nodded deferentially, bringing up his data slate and transmitting a selection of documents via near field communication. "You'll want to look at this before you go down and scare that poor man to death."

"Aww," Heavy Dub complained. "Can I still scare him, just a little?"

Albert smiled. "You totally can, after you've read these documents."

Brook read the documents, at four times the speed of a human, and with perfect photographic clarity. Sliding the data slate back into her rucksack she slid her goggles up so Albert could see her silvery eyes. He looked back, nodding sympathetically.

"They take Kale, and then ask for a favor? I want to hurt people, Albert," Brook said, gently putting a hand on his arm.

"If they are here asking for our help, it is far more likely that Kale is *taking them*. Look at it as aggressively sealing a business deal," Albert said, reassuring her.

"Why wouldn't he tell us?" Heavy Dub said.

"So your reactions would seem genuine, your outrage as real as possible. Now, go down and scare the crap out of that representative of the Mexican government, and make it look good," Albert said, nodding to Heavy Dub.

"Ohmygodyes!" Heavy Dub said, clapping while he jumped from one foot to the other, excitedly.

Five floors down, Captain Oleastro checked his watch, hoping he wouldn't have to wear the same clothes for another day. He went over the offer in his head again, making sure all the documents were in order, and that he'd remembered to bring his diplomatic credentials with him. He sipped the coffee Albert Tensman's secretary brought him an hour ago, wondering how Uroboros Financial had managed to get their hands on real coffee beans.

Brook opened the door so hard it flew off the hinges, bending the metal commercial frame that once held it up. Captain Oleastro looked up, startled, as Heavy Dub stomped in behind her, his face betraying none of the mirth it had held a moment ago. Brook flicked the conference table aside with one hand, sending it into the wall, and stormed up to Captain Oleastro. Brook grabbed him up by the lapels and held him aloft.

"What is the meaning of this? I'm waiting for the CEO of Uroboros Financial. I have diplomatic..."

Brook interrupted him, pressing him against the wall with one hand, the other holding a single finger over his mouth. He could see his own eyes reflected back at him in the lenses of her goggles, an expression that quickly turned to fear. Her grip was like the hardest steel, and the cybernetically enhanced man behind her seemed to take a sadistic pleasure in watching him squirm.

"I am her," Brook said, her lips moving like a pair of snakes, fighting to the death, before being violently separated by clenched teeth.

Captain Oleastro tried to reply, but Brook held him fast.

"How you want to do this? Send him back to the Mexican consulate in pieces?" Heavy Dub asked.

"I don't know. I'm so angry right now…" Brook said, for Oleastro's benefit, taking a deep breath. "That doesn't seem bad enough. It doesn't convey how badly they've messed up," Brook said, pushing Captain Oleastro's head from side to side slowly, hand clamped tightly over his mouth.

Captain Oleastro gesticulated wildly, pointing to the fallen folder of documents he'd brought with him.

"Yeah, I saw your government's offer. You need our help. You need… my help," Brook said, smiling, her mouth open slightly, the pronounced canines granted by her Drone heritage protruding sharply.

Captain Oleastro nodded, vigorously.

"You remember those reports of orbital strikes across Europe and North Africa? Brook has a friend that made that happen with a text message. Sending you back to the consulate in a tiny diplomatically sealed envelope is the least of the really bad shit Brook is about to do to Mexico," Heavy Dub said, leaning casually against the wall beside where Oleastro was pinned.

Oleastro began praying, his eyes turning skyward, his hands clasped in front of him. Brook enjoyed frightening him far too much, feeling some of herself go in dark delight. It would be easy to kill him, and she wasn't sure she wouldn't enjoy it immensely.

Heavy Dub looked down at the floor, then back up at Brook. "He pissed himself."

"I'm not pretending, Heavy Dub. This isn't an act. Not anymore," Brook said, breathing heavily, eyes wide with fright as terrible impulses flooded her being.

"Think this through. Take a minute," Heavy Dub said, looking on, and becoming genuinely worried.

"Maybe if I scare them bad enough, hurt them bad enough, they'll give him back," Brook said, taking her hand off his mouth, and drawing her hammer menacingly from the hanger at her side.

"Kale sent me here. He made all this happen," Oleastro blurted out, closing his eyes and wincing.

Brook smiled. "You'd say anything to save yourself. Anything. It won't work. You are dead." Brook's smile vanished. "Dead."

"Um, I'm voting to give this guy sixty seconds to explain," Heavy Dub said, putting a firm metallic hand on Brook's shoulder.

Brook pressed in, making it hard for Oleastro to breathe, the pressure cracking the drywall around him. "On Mars, I hear there are Company Operators that can vivisect a man way past the bone, and all the while keeping them alive to feel everything. I'm a type 3ES, and I am very good at detecting lies. You'll get your sixty seconds, but if you lie to me, even once, I will put you in a stasis chamber and ship you to Mars."

Oleastro nodded feverishly. "I understand."

Brook set him down slowly, holstering her hammer at her side. Oleastro watched as she slid her goggles up, revealing a smooth and alluring face that framed fierce silver eyes. She would be lovely, he thought, but her expression was marred by terrible pain, and endless sadness. He'd heard that Drones had emotional capacities far beyond humans with regard to those they considered part of their tribe, but had never seen it in person before.

"Kale wants you to join him in Mexico as soon as possible. He manufactured a way for you to come over. The Mexican government is begging to have you, and anyone you deem essential, in the envoy that comes over," Oleastro said, rubbing the bruises rising up around his neck.

"So, you guys messed with Kale, and then he bent you over a barrel?" Heavy Dub said, laughing.

"That was the Cartel. There is a silent civil war going on in Mexico. The legitimately elected government needs a way to provide jobs, and occupy transportation companies, to dull the allure of the Cartel's global operations," Oleastro explained. "Kale has contrived a way to make that happen."

"These diplomatic credentials are fresh. My nose can still detect the oxidation taking place as the ink is absorbed into the paper," Brook said, scooping his documents up off the floor.

Oleastro looked incredulous at the comment, blinking at Brook, and then over at Heavy Dub.

Heavy Dub laughed. "I can't fart on the other side of the building without her sending me a nasty gram via our mobiles. If she says the ink is fresh, that's exactly what it is."

Oleastro swallowed nervously, and nodded. "Kale insisted that I be the one to act on the government's behalf. I haven't been in possession of my diplomatic capacities for more than a week."

"Why?" Brook asked, angrily hurling Oleastro's credentials at him.

"I'm the one who made the exchange in Montana, and transported the personnel and assets that he has safely sequestered across the border. I've been his man in Mexico for months," Oleastro said, making sure Brook could see his face clearly.

Brook watched him say the words, playing them back in her mind over and over, observing every microexpression and vocal component. "He's not lying, or he doesn't think he is," Brook said, looking to Heavy Dub.

"Goddamn, Kale is sneaky," Heavy Dub said, nodding approvingly.

"We never thought this contingency would be needed, and that Mexico could handle these problems internally. Outsiders have gotten involved, making certain assets important to the Cartel, eh, very desperate. Kale didn't want any of this to happen, or for this plan to be necessary," Oleastro explained.

"Prove it," Brook said, frowning.

"He thought you might need more proof than simply my word, and your ability to detect falsehoods. He told me to have you check the range logs here at the firm. That they would give you what you need," Oleastro said, not sure himself how that would provide Brook with the proof she needed.

Brook pulled out her data slate and checked the logs. Kale hadn't been training with just his usual trio of weapons that he preferred. He'd also spent weeks familiarizing himself with a dozen different weapons known to be used by the Mexican military, and the criminal Cartel that opposed them. Brook slowly lifted her eyes, an angry scowl crossing her face.

"Can I see?" Heavy Dub asked.

Brook handed him the data slate. "What does Kale want us to do next?"

Oleastro nodded, glad he might make it through the day alive. "Gather an envoy for the mission in question, and make it look as legitimate as possible. I think he wants the right people present if no negotiation can be reached. Your friend, Kale, is very mysterious."

"These are cool guns. Except that one. Never really liked that one," Heavy Dub murmured, gazing at the range logs.

"I'm an extremely valuable commodity on the black market in Mexico. How are we going to secure the safety of the citizenry while I'm there," Brook asked.

"Well… you mean, or, don't you mean, how will we secure your safety?" Oleastro said, not fully understanding.

"That's not what she means," Heavy Dub said, as Brook rested her hand on her hammer. "There isn't an enhanced combatant classification for someone like her. She's personnel loss, and property damage plus, times a hundred, or something."

"I don't understand," Oleastro replied.

"I watched her hit a full conversion cyborg with her hammer in Italy. The lady in question had full ablative armor, reinforced with an aperiodic carbon weave mesh. 20 millimeter rounds would just knock her around. Brook killed her with a single hit," Heavy Dub explained, eyebrows high on his forehead.

"God, okay. Hopefully, we can keep your presence a secret. The Mexican government and the Cartel don't want the bad press, as this is a battle for hearts and minds. Having Brook engaging armed aggressors on the streets isn't good for anyone," Oleastro said, nodding.

Brook closed her eyes. "Is he safe?"

Oleastro hesitated to respond, not sure how she would react. "No one in Mexico is safe."

Brook covered her face, tears flowing freely as frustration and worry took its toll.

"Brook, it's just another disaster zone. People are trapped inside. It's time to do what we do best," Heavy Dub said, steadying her.

"I wouldn't send myself on this mission. I wouldn't because I'm compromised emotionally. My hierarchy of values won't work when Kale is trapped inside," Brook concluded.

"Every job is just a job," Heavy Dub said, quoting Perfidy.

"As soon as it wasn't, Perfidy got himself killed," Brook said, the words bringing little comfort.

"He died so others wouldn't have to. That old man died with no regrets, doing what he loved, with the people he loved. Remember that," Heavy Dub said, assured.

"Millions of lives are hanging in the balance. What little of the world that is still trying to rise out of the chaos will be cut in half if you do not act," Oleastro said, gathering paperwork from the floor.

"Silverstein and Ezra One let historically unprecedented chaos happen to save just one person they cared about. Once, I couldn't understand why they did that. I get it now," Brook said, exiting the wrecked conference room.

CHAPTER 3

MONTERREY, NUEVO LEÓN, MEXICO – PALACIO DEL OBISPADO

SEPTEMBER 10TH, 2201 – 2:17 PM

Kale picked up his coffee, cradling the saucer in one hand while holding the handle on the cup with the other. The aroma of the coffee seemed to push out everything else, helping him clear away unwanted and distracting thoughts. Across the table from him was an empty chair, but he expected it to be filled soon.

The café wasn't busy. There were a few regulars, a handful of tourists, and an old man Kale kept a wary eye on. The coffee was delicious, the beans fresh, and recently roasted to very exacting standards. Kale pushed the silver tray of sugar, crème, and other additives away, as if even their presence was insulting the coffee's flavor.

Silverstein arrived, waved his way past the staff, and found his way to the chair opposite Kale. He took a silken napkin and laid it across his lap. He raised his hand to order, the waiter rushing over with notepad and pen in hand.

"I'll have what he's having," Silverstein said, gesturing to Kale.

"We tend to like the same things," Silverstein and Kale said, in unison.

The waiter paused, struck by how similar the two men looked, and yet, how different. "Yes, sir. I'll bring it straight away."

Silverstein was bedraggled, tired, but clean cut, and wearing a light gray suit with a blue tie. Kale's hair was long, his beard cut down to stubble, and he wore a tailored black suit, long coat, and sported an emerald green tie. Silverstein looked anxious, bereft of rest, while Kale looked calm, without any hint of worry, or duress.

"You look terrible," Kale said, looking at him through the steam coming off his cup.

"I spent a few days in a Mexican military black site," Silverstein replied, rubbing his face with his hands.

"That is awful."

"Without my socks."

"Barbaric. Did you find what we were looking for?" Kale asked, unsympathetically.

"No. Yes. Maybe."

Kale nodded, picking up the local paper. It was tied off with string, freshly picked flowers tucked within. Silverstein watched as Kale opened it, took the flowers out, and placed them in a short vase with water on the table.

"Do they do that at all the tables?" Silverstein asked, watching Kale methodically arrange the flowers.

"Just mine, apparently," Kale said, looking over at the tables immediately nearby.

Silverstein sighed. "I'm sorry you were drawn into this. I hoped, especially after what happened in Europe, that you wouldn't have to..."

"Stop apologizing to me," Kale whispered harshly, his coffee cup clacking down against the saucer.

Silverstein almost blurted out another apology, but thought better of it. "Is Brook coming?"

"Are we going to have that conversation?" Kale said, meeting Silverstein's gaze for the first time. "Here? Now?"

Silverstein sat back in his chair, inhaling sharply. He tried to blink away the moment, but Kale persisted to be there in front of him, his cold stare boring holes through him. He'd never considered the aftermath of crafting replicas, or that one would go delta to the degree that Kale had.

It was like the proverbial devil on the shoulder, but with Kale, there was no angel as a counterweight. He'd become dangerous and powerful in ways that the older, and wiser, Silverstein had declined to become. Like Silverstein, Kale was a person of deeply held principles, and while Silverstein suspected they were not so different from his own, they might be different enough.

"No, not unless you want to," Silverstein said at last, nodding to the waiter as he brought more coffee to the table.

"You sound like a therapist when you say it like that. You know how I feel about mental health professionals," Kale said, upper lip curling disdainfully as Silverstein added cream to his coffee.

"Wow, you are really angry," Silverstein said, a little shocked.

"It amuses me to make you think so," Kale said, savoring his coffee while he watched Silverstein gulp down his. "In truth, I do not blame you for this, whatsoever."

Silverstein nodded, feeling relieved. "You need someone in the room to think there's a rift between us. You're protecting me."

Kale looked down at the newspaper, showing no emotion. "I am protecting *us*."

"Okay, so, are we going with your plan, or mine?" Silverstein asked, fighting the urge to look around the room.

"We can try your plan, first. It is a better plan, admittedly. That said, be prepared to adapt," Kale replied, neatly folding the newspaper and replacing it on the table.

Silverstein paused, looking down at the table. "And, what was my plan again?"

"The Mexican government needs jobs, particularly those to satiate the teamsters unions. They need to undermine the Cartels, and give the people financial incentive to support them," Kale replied, turning the newspaper over, and sliding it to Silverstein.

Silverstein looked down at the newspaper, reading the upturned headline. "Ah."

"Mexico wants to spread across the world, rebuilding it, while bringing to it their own brand of enlightened democracy. They cannot do that without a steady and safe supply of raw materials," Kale said, looking past Silverstein to the old man watching them.

Silverstein took a deep breath. "Mars."

"Yes, but there is a problem."

"Mars doesn't trust Mexico. They haven't for decades," Silverstein said, closing his eyes, and feeling guilty.

"You did your best. Both you and Ezra One. Do you know what you get if you mix orange and teal?" Kale asked, turning his coffee cup clockwise on the saucer.

"No. We never had to find out," Silverstein replied, wondering how Kale knew as much as he did.

Kale nodded. "And, how did you accomplish that?"

"I think you know already."

Kale clasped his hands together, placing them on the table. "Do you have the stomach for it again?"

"I didn't back then, but that must be somewhat obvious by now," Silverstein said, closing his eyes and hugging his own shoulders.

"It was courage and faith in people that led you to that conclusion back then," Kale said, reaching across the table and retrieving his newspaper. "It was kindness."

"How do we do that again?" Silverstein asked, opening his eyes. "How do we do this without killing her? How does Vivian survive this?"

"Like I said, we go with your plan," Kale said, opening the paper and looking at the sports page with great interest.

Silverstein chuckled sadly. "I guess I better figure out what that is."

Kale pressed his lips together tightly, already pulling together all the variables, and possible outcomes. He didn't have the computing power of a full Cabal Numismatist, but he could see Silverstein was troubled. He couldn't see a way out for everyone, a way that Mexico didn't bleed badly from the wound it had inflicted upon itself.

Silverstein knew more than he was telling, about Vivian, Doctor Madmar, and Kaspersky. He'd only recently discovered more of the truth, but even in that, he barely allowed himself to believe it. The horror of it all was still too fresh to process, too close to his heart to bear up into the complexity of his mind. He would have to sit on it a little bit longer, for everyone's sake.

"The more we meddle in affairs not our own, the worse it will be," Silverstein concluded.

"Do you think we have any power to influence what Mexico's people will decide to do? We are ants under the foot of a titan. They endured the Shut Down, and prospered in the wake of it," Kale said, smiling faintly at the coffee held in his hand.

"I'm not talking about that. How do you know about Mars? That was decades ago," Silverstein asked.

"That is a sensitive conversation, and we have an audience."

Silverstein nodded. "We need a proper analogue, then."

"Have you heard the story of Anchises?" Kale asked, looking up at the fresco painted on the ceiling overhead.

"He's warned not to boast of his affair with Aphrodite, lest he be struck by a thunderbolt. In the version you're referring to, was he killed, or merely rendered blind?" Silverstein replied, shifting uncomfortably.

"What matters is that he had a son," Kale replied, sipping his coffee. "That son, Aeneas, had a wife. In carrying his elderly father out of the flames of Troy, his wife did not survive as they escaped."

"But, the son of Aeneas and Creusa, Ascanius, would survive to be part of the lineage of Romulus, the founder of Rome," Silverstein said.

"Anchises' foolish pride nearly got his son and grandson killed. Creusa pleaded with them to flee. To think of their posterity. The Gods set her aflame as a sign, along with a shooting star. At last Anchises, dousing Creusa in water, agrees to flee Troy," Kale replies, squinting upward.

Silverstein nodded. "She does not die then, but later as she falters behind as they flee, presumably killed by the Greeks."

"Aeneas goes back to find her, but she has been killed, or taken. Then, Creusa's ghost appears, telling him where he will go, and that he will marry another. She pleads with him to care for their son," Kale said, setting his coffee down, and folding his arms.

"And, Aeneas tries to hold her three times, but cannot take hold of her before she vanishes into the ether," Silverstein says, beginning to understand. "She was rescued, in death, by Rhea and Aphrodite to keep her from being enslaved."

Kale nodded, giving Silverstein a hardened expression.

"Except in our version of the story, I'm Anchises, I got Aeneas killed, hid Ascanius away, and I am the one haunted by Creusa?" Silverstein muttered, shaking his head. "How do we deal with her?"

Kale cocked his head to one side, "Do you really see yourself as Anchises?"

"If not me, then who?" Silverstein replied, sullenly.

"Doctor Maurice Madmar. I know you see him as a victim, but I am confident that regardless of his role, what happened was not your fault," Kale said, his expression darkening with his mood.

"What are you seeing in this that I can't?" Silverstein asked.

"It may be that as much as we need to address the plight of Creusa, we need to appeal to the desires of Rhea and Aphrodite."

"Did you lay awake all night thinking of that analogue?" Silverstein said, covering his face with his hands.

"It is good, no?"

"Yes, it's pretty good," Silverstein said, a slim grin crossing his face.

"I assume this explains why we are going with your plan, and not with mine," Kale replied, checking the time on his mobile.

"You can't kill what is already dead," Silverstein said, pouring himself more coffee.

"There are so many things worse than death. So many states of being in this world that make death appear as the glow of the Elysian Fields, as opposed to shadows of Hades. It is creating for people the proper perspective that must become our task," Kale said, quietly delighting in the look of consternation slowly growing on the old man's face sitting across the café.

"It is the noblest task," Silverstein said, nodding. "Can you bring Ascanius to us? If needed?"

Kale nodded. "I don't know."

Silverstein gave Kale a blank stare, as it was rare that Kale ever possessed any incertitude of things.

"Custody orders that cross borders are tricky enough. Ascanius is currently in the protective custody of one of the few sworn law enforcement officers in North America," Kale said, putting his hands behind his head and leaning back in his chair.

"I know about all that. This isn't about paperwork, is it?" Silverstein said, nodding.

"Everyone who has tried to take Ascanius from Ursa Major is in Hades, or in the process of being sent to the shadow of Ares," Kale said, delighting privately in keeping the analogue going.

"Does Ursa Major answer to anyone?" Silverstein asked.

"He, and our girl with a hammer, share a special bond, but she will not do what you're thinking of asking."

Silverstein rubbed his temples and closed his eyes, losing himself in thought.

The lights flickered, casting the cafe beneath the fresco into darkness. When the emergency lights came up, Kale was on his feet, standing beside the table with the older man that had been observing Kale and Silverstein converse. Kale revealed a handgun hidden beneath his jacket, making sure that only the elderly man could see it.

"Leave," Kale said, tapping the grip on his handgun with one hand, while gesturing toward the door with the other. "I suspect you will have more pressing matters to attend to anyway."

The older man dashed out, pausing at the doorway adjoining a patio. One could see the whole city of Monterrey below, block by block, building by building, the power going out across the city. Red repossession lights flicked on above doorways and in cars. The entire city was being Shut Down.

Silverstein watched Kale return to the table, taking his seat and swirling what remained of his coffee at the bottom of the cup. The wait staff scrambled to try and salvage the situation, customers rising from their seats to complain. Silverstein looked at his mobile. The local network was down, but he still had connectivity via satellite, his ally, Selene AI, granting him access to the global grid.

"Our seamstress must have just arrived," Kale said, drinking the last of his coffee.

"She's early," Silverstein replied, nodding. "I guess I should go. Traffic will be terrible."

"I think you will have all kinds of time. It is likely that our girl with a hammer called the seamstress when she was given clearance to come to Mexico. Discovering that they were both coming here, they probably decided to come at the same time," Kale said, trying to flag down a waiter.

"Yes, sir?" a waiter said, looking worried.

"Just more coffee, before it gets cold," Kale said.

"Is that all?" the waiter said, relieved.

"Please," Kale said, handing off his coffee cup.

Silverstein looked up at the fresco overhead. It was new, part of the more recent Muralism Movement in Latin America. It was a take on the Sistine Chapel, but not a copy of the fresco inside. It depicted the building itself, as a sort of source of light. The background was full of cherubs and the wind of trumpet blasts obscured in and around the shadows of the structure.

In the building around them there was a certain mathematical symmetry that became apparent. The place, like so many others, was probably an older haven of the Cabal, both in form and spirit. The place echoed of old things for Silverstein. He hoped that someday, he could find a place where nothing within reminded him of the past.

"I'm glad they are friends," Silverstein said, opening a packet of crackers he had stashed in a jacket pocket.

"Was this an unexpected outcome?" Kale said, gesturing to the darkened city outside the window.

"It couldn't have been the Mexican government, and the Cartel should know better as well. Our seamstress and I haven't talked much lately, so I don't know who else might be in her entourage," Silverstein said, worriedly.

Kale nodded to the waiter bringing him a fresh cup of coffee. "You're worried she brought Marjorie?"

Silverstein blinked. "Oh, I hadn't even considered that. I hope not."

"Are you not curious what will happen if those two start spending time with one another?" Kale asked, frowning again as Silverstein added crème and sugar to the coffee he had been neglecting.

"I don't know that either one of them has the minute control over their abilities required for that to be safe," Silverstein said, checking his mobile to see there was a text message from Taylor.

"You worry too much," Kale said, smiling in a way that made Silverstein uncomfortable.

"It's a perpetual state when you've lived as long as I have. My mind creates a statistical model for how things can go wrong, and I've seen more outcomes than most," Silverstein said, hoping Marjorie was still on walkabout.

"It is simply another reason to use your plan," Kale said, bowing his head.

"While I'm trying to make peace, what are you going to do?" Silverstein asked.

"Kill everyone who tries to stop you," Kale said, closing his eyes and bowing his head further.

"Let's be reasonable, I can talk to him, and..."

Kale shook his head. "No, you cannot."

"What would our girl with a hammer say about this? I think you should..."

"Shut your mouth," Kale said, his eyes flying open to glare harshly at Silverstein across the table.

Silverstein swallowed, but he couldn't stomach the fear he felt. Whatever inkling Kale had, it was bad, bad enough he was holding it inside so it would not darken anyone else. It was the worst sort of dread. Silverstein knew it well, as he had kept many dangerous secrets of the same sort, for thousands of years.

"I trust you, Kale. You and I are the same. If you feel like it has to be this way, I probably would as well. I'm sorry for questioning you."

"It is fine. You are, of course, correct. We should move toward our goals no more quickly than is needed. Go, meet our seamstress at the airport before the local repossession protocol snarls traffic even worse.

Talk to Rhea, and Aphrodite, see if they can be reasoned with," Kale said, annoyed at himself for losing his temper.

"I might have a mutual associate do that, given his special relationship with one of them," Silverstein said, nodding.

"Then, make sure you talk to the other. All of my success swaying the Gods, came from following your example," Kale said, standing up and shaking Silverstein's hand.

Kale watched Silverstein amble out into the foyer, acting naturally, and with the same degree of bafflement at the outage afflicting the city. He wasn't gone long before Kale's second appointment arrived. Gelt Burkholder strolled in wearing casual North American street clothes beneath a very expensive long coat. His hair was long enough to rival Kale's but he was clean shaven, his old hat held in his hand.

"I like the beard," Gelt said, sitting down.

Kale's cold expression didn't change. The sight of Gelt enraged him to the degree he had to dig his fingernails into his palm to distract him from the hate and loathing he felt. He felt like his teeth would break if they were clenched together any tighter.

He thought of Brook. He replayed the sounds she made on the odd morning he could sleep in. She would bustle about their small apartment, tidying things, pressing shirts, and making breakfast. She would hum, perfectly in tune while she did it, a rare thing among Drones. They so rarely had the opportunity to listen to music in the underground.

They could afford better, and she didn't need to clean a single dish or tidy a single square foot of flooring with the old straw broom she preferred. They'd decided to live simply, without distraction, so they could focus entirely on the time they had alone together. His affection for her made him dangerous, because deep down, he was just like Silverstein. He'd let the world burn, before he'd let anything happen to someone he loved.

"Stepfather," Kale said calmly, offering some coffee from the kettle on the table, pushing a clean cup over to him.

"How'd the talk with Ouroboru go?" Gelt asked, regarding the no smoking sign with some sadness.

"We are, strangely, always of one mind," Kale replied, an easy smile crossing his face.

Gelt smirked. "Didn't seem like it from where I was sitting,"

"You were watching?" Kale said, quietly glad the earlier display had a proper audience.

"The whole thing. So, how about you keep yours in the holster under your left arm, and I keep mine at my hip. Sound good?" Gelt said, patting the handgun at his side.

Kale nodded. "Sounds good."

"You Deltas are dangerous and unpredictable, so set me at ease," Gelt said.

"I promise, my pistol will stay in the holster," Kale said, nodding respectfully.

"I understand you're angry, but I'm not entirely sure why. Whatever it is, I'm sure we can work it out," Gelt said, holding his hands out toward Kale, as if to offer up his non-apology in a more palatable way.

"What makes you think I am angry?" Kale asked, holding his breath to listen to the chaos going on outside as people scrambled in the dark, trying to figure out how they would get home.

The Palacio Del Obispado wasn't too remote, but with every vehicle and cab afflicted by repossession protocols, people would simply have to walk, lacking transportation insulated from the citywide phenomenon. It was a walk most of the affluent patrons were unwilling to accept without complaint. Kale quietly delighted in their discomfort as the staff of the Palacio did their best to pacify them with free rooms and drinks.

"I could always tell. Although, to be honest, this level of anger always got leveled at your stepmother," Gelt said, pouring himself some coffee from the table.

"She bore the brunt of it because she was strong enough to take it. I was always afraid I would irreparably shatter your fragile heart," Kale said, his upper lip curling with disgust.

"Goddamn, boy, what did I do to you? That attempted snatch and grab up in the Dakotas? All I was trying to do was get you clear of it all, while I do what needs to be done," Gelt said, fidgeting with his cigarettes.

"You said you were watching Silverstein and me the whole time?" Kale said, leaning back in his chair.

"Yes, but I didn't understand any of what you were talking about. Classical myth wasn't a prerequisite for what the tribe asked me to do for the Cabal," Gelt said, squinting at Kale.

"Is that a fact?" Kale said, shrugging.

"And, who was that old guy that you threatened and ran out of the hotel? He wasn't one of mine. Mexican military intelligence?" Gelt asked, looking around for the waiter after discovering the coffee had gone cold.

"Just someone I paid to make it look good," Kale said, smirking.

"Hey, when the lights went out, did you and Silverstein change places?" Gelt said, looking down at the table with a look of consternation.

"We did," Kale said, calmly shooting Gelt under the table.

Gelt flew backwards, hand on his pistol but he quickly felt paralysis ravaging his body, radiating outward from the wound in his gut. Kale stood calmly, watching bemused as the patrons ran for their lives. He knelt down next to Gelt, an ancient .45 caliber 1911 held in his hand.

Gelt squinted, struggling to even raise his head. "That's Silverstein's gun. He hasn't used it since the second World War."

"You are new at this, so you could not possibly have known what I'm about to tell you. Nanotechnological replicas, older ones particularly, can detect one another. Even if we are not a replica of the same person. Something in the eyes," Kale explained.

"What..."

"Maybe, you do not realize what you are. You do not have my stepfather's memories, certainly not all of them. His farmhouse is full of books on classical myth, and he labored for the Cabal as their master scribe before being released in the fifteen hundreds, and replaced by Cal. The analogue would have been an easy code for my real stepfather to crack," Kale explained, calmly holding the 1911 up in front of Gelt so he could see the empty chamber, slide back.

"The rest of the magazine is empty," Gelt said, looking up at the holster that had been hastily fastened to the underside of the table. "Why all the trouble?"

"I have questions, things that you might know, but that Gelt would never willingly tell Silverstein, or me," Kale said, stowing the pistol under his coat.

"You're going to try and get me to break away, go Delta, like you?" Gelt said, smiling weakly.

"There was only one bullet because that particular one is very hard to make. It was coated with particles about twenty nanometers in diameter. They are incorporated with a powerful photosensitive molecule, and coated with a polyethylene shell. It is small enough to dodge even your advanced immune system, and slowly excite various other molecules in your body," Kale explained. "Are you feeling hot yet?"

"Yes," Gelt said, beginning to sweat profusely.

"The rapid oxidation, accompanied with the heat you are feeling, and even the little light in the room around us, will cause your body to slowly succumb to combustion, burning you slowly from the outside in," Kale said, calmly gesturing to the gut wound Gelt barely had the strength to keep pressure on.

"Fascinating," Gelt said, sweat pouring down into his eyes.

"If I get you to a dark and cold place quickly enough, the process will slow, and eventually your body will flush the nanoparticles out naturally. The walk-in freezer in the kitchen of this hotel would be sufficient," Kale said, sitting down cross-legged beside Gelt.

"And if you don't?" Gelt asked.

"My curiosity about how this particular weapon works on nanotechnologically contrived replicas will be sated. I imagine it is a pretty bad death, but spectacular at the same time. Do feel free to relate your own observations to me while it is happening," Kale said, taking in a sharp cleansing breath as the café grew quiet at last.

Gelt closed his eyes. "What do you want to know?"

"Why was Kaspersky killing those children and preserving them as dolls? Why did the Cabal allow it to happen?" Kale asked.

"He was crazy, no one knows why he was doing that," Gelt said.

"I should drag you into the foyer where there is more light. It will help you remember," Kale said, reaching down and taking hold of Gelt's lapels.

"They were the children of the tribe," Gelt blurted out. "And, their descendants."

"Explain," Kale said, setting Gelt back down on the ground.

"Having an alien fill you with implants derived from the science of quantum biology had risks. Not every myth about mad gods and monsters came entirely from the mind of a poet. Bogumil commanded everyone to remain celibate, or handle the task of getting rid of any offspring that came from not being so," Gelt explained, laying back so sweat would cease rolling into his eyes.

"It was an institutional control within the Cabal," Kale concluded, shaking his head in disgust.

"Yes."

"Kaspersky was tasked with handling slip ups, and sentimental missteps, while Golgotha did her best to police the Cabal around the fringes," Kale said, more to affirm what he already suspected, than as a declaration of discovery.

"Not everyone was cut out to kill their own offspring just because the patron of our power said so. It felt unfair that we would harbor her children in our own bodies, while not allowed to have any of our own. It didn't take even a handful of centuries for the resentment to grow. Not everyone had a child, like Bogumil, that could be a companion over the course of many millennia," Gelt said, beginning to breathe harder.

"Why did Kaspersky go after Doctor Madmar?" Kale asked, keeping an eye on the exits, a little surprised Gelt's replica had come alone.

Gelt laughed. "You watched the tape?"

"Yes."

"Ask yourself who he was really going after."

Kale shook his head, cold rage building up inside him. "Vivian. What about the madness that jumped across the man-machine interface from Kaspersky, to Maurice Madmar, and..."

"Exposure to the energies generated by alien quantum biological implants is bad for the mind. Also, consider what's in Kaspersky's mind, all he's seen... and done. A glimpse is all you'd need to go completely mad," Gelt said, nodding.

"You kept all of this from us?" Kale said, visibly angry.

"Ouroboru was one of a handful that followed Bogumil's edict. He stayed dutifully celibate, and was released, several times, via our amnestic traditions. There was never a reason for him to know," Gelt explained, the skin on the back of his hands beginning to glow.

"Like you and my stepmother," Kale said, frowning.

"It's not like, in her case, she had a fucking choice," Gelt said, the sensation of burning across his exposed skin growing more intense.

"Yes, all very tragic. The difference is that you, and Cerise, Archie, and half the militant arm of the Cabal, all tried to capitalize on your immortality instead of staying focused on the task. Only we stayed the course. Only we were truly devoted to saving the world," Kale said, slapping Gelt lightly on the face to keep him conscious.

"We did what was necessary," Gelt rasped, struggling to breathe.

"Necessity is the poorest of reasons to do anything. You are either the ever-elusive 'good boy' bereft of the responsibility to make real decisions, or the eternally penitent sinner, with only the illusion of choice. You never see beyond what the world does to you, or the savage impulses that tug within. Reason is the crown of humanity, and I see in you only the most barren brow," Kale whispered.

"Fair enough. So what now? You show me the ways of being a Delta, and we join forces?" Gelt said, shifting uncomfortably. "How about that walk-in freezer you were talking about?"

"No. Like you said before, Deltas are dangerous and unpredictable," Kale said, drawing his own sidearm and shooting Gelt in the forehead.

CHAPTER 4

MONTERREY, NUEVO LEÓN, MEXICO – PALACIO DEL OBISPADO

SEPTEMBER 10TH, 2201 – 2:17 PM

Taylor struggled with her bag, the bountiful contents making it hard to remove from the overhead compartment. She unzipped the large over-stuffed bag, moving the contents around so that the bag could be freed from the bin. Others exiting the flight milled past her, with a few offering to help her with her bag along the way.

"No, no, I got this," Taylor said, declining each offer.

After a valiant struggle, she was able to pull it free, setting it down just as a steward on board the transport was coming to give her some assistance. "Thanks, I got it."

"Hey, your brother really took off after the flight landed. Everything all right?" The steward asked, looking through bins, and between seats for anything people forgot to take with them.

Taylor observed her for a moment, just long enough to get a feel for whether she was being nice, or prying for information. The last few days made her paranoid enough to question anyone. Her uniform seemed to fit, worn in the right places, a few places hand sewn with thread that was close in color to the fabric, but not quite right. She seemed calm, like a person would be when they were just making conversation.

"Yeah, he had an important meeting to get to. The flight was twenty minutes late," Taylor replied, slinging her brightly colored bag over her shoulder.

The steward nodded, continuing to do her post-flight sweep. Stooping down, Taylor could see there were several official looking men waiting in the port. They were carefully observing the passengers as they came out. She couldn't be sure if they were looking for her, or just looking.

"Only one way to find out," Taylor whispered, taking a deep breath.

She walked, keeping her head down, and the hood on her colorful jacket up. The men ceased their scrutiny of everyone else the moment she appeared, their collective gaze resting on her. Taylor swallowed, pausing at the bottom of the personnel loading ramp.

The tallest among them wore a black suit, a copper colored shirt, and a white tie. His hair was cut close, like he was military, but his hands were smooth, like he'd never worked a hard day in his life. He unbuttoned his jacket and approached Taylor in a way that made him seem courteous, until he spoke.

"You constitute a forbidden technology. You aren't even a person in Mexico. We're going to have to confiscate you," he said.

"If I'm not even a person, why are you talking to me? Do you yell at your toaster in the morning? Have lengthy conversations with door knobs? You sound ridiculous," Taylor said, laughing.

"I assume something like you has monitoring of some sort. I'm speaking more out of courtesy, so that when whoever owns you and finds that you're in custody, they will know why," the man said, showing his credentials.

Taylor laughed. "No one owns me."

"It's amazing how real you seem. If you're capable of knowing any-thing, you should have known better than to come here," the man said, gesturing for his men to come forward.

"It's Cortes, right? Pizarro Cortes?" Taylor ventured, her hair streaking with white as she spoke.

Cortes turned his head to one side, staring at her angrily. "How do you know that?"

"The government ID card you just put back in your pocket has radio frequency identification technology built into it. It took me a week to learn how to do it, but I can mimic the electromagnetic field of an interrogator unit. I know who all of you are, thanks to the ID cards you carry," Taylor said, smiling warmly.

"This is probably why you constitute a banned technology in Mexico," Cortes said.

"I have diplomatic papers, and represent the Lunar Colony. I'd like to go about my business, please," Taylor said, remaining polite and composed.

"We don't recognize anyone that doesn't have a consulate here, and a formal diplomatic relationship with Mexico," Cortes said, motioning for his men to take Taylor into custody.

They grabbed her arms, one of them taking her bag from her. They set the bag on the deck and began looking through it. Cortes pulled out his mobile to send a text, but he couldn't find a signal.

Taylor wasn't sure what she was going to do. She assumed there might be some trouble at customs, but nothing like this. That's when she could feel it, running like black ink through the white ice of everything electronic around her.

It had been a year since she'd felt that particular machine language, or heard the whisper of it. She had spoken to her mother and several other artificial intelligences in her quest to find the source of it, but to no avail. It was supposed to reset the world, right the global economy, and halt the cycle of debt and death that afflicted everyone.

Now, it was loose in Monterrey, shutting everything down.

"This is your last chance. Let me go," Taylor said, looking over at the men that had taken her by the arms.

Cortes gave his mobile a funny look before pocketing it. "Any of you have a signal?"

"No, they don't," Taylor replied. The dye in her hair went from green and blue to the color of bleached bone with each passing moment.

Cortes held out his hand to one of his men, gesturing to the holster at his side. The man drew his sidearm, unlocked it with a biometric sensor, and handed it to him. Cortes checked the chamber to make sure it was ready to fire and leveled it at Taylor, holding the barrel an inch from her cheek.

"I need to make a call," Cortes said, calmly moving his finger from the guard to the trigger.

"I'm sorry about all this," Taylor said, shaking her head. "You should have let me go."

The port went dark, the electrical hum of powered loading ramps going silent. Conveyors moving baggage and people ground to a halt, as the entire port lost power. The electronic countermeasures in the weapons of every security guard, intelligence agent, and police officer tripped, rendering their weapons useless. Vehicles of every kind went into repossession protocols, giving drivers and crew sixty seconds to evacuate before they locked up tight.

Emergency lighting struggled to flicker on, as cries of alarm and fright rose up from the baggage claim and security checkpoints. Cortes pulled the trigger on the gun, but the governmental safety mechanism in it had been tripped as well. Taylor glowed dimly in the aftermath, her dark skin giving off a faint luminescence. The men backed away from her, hand held up in fright.

"My mom hoped that a gesture of goodwill would be enough. That the moon and Mexico could be allies in this," Taylor said, the glow around her slowly fading as the color in her hair bled back through.

"My government won't deal with you. We'll figure out how to regain control of the port," Cortes said, grabbing Taylor by the throat.

"May seventeenth of last year, do you remember that day?" Taylor asked.

Cortes nodded, immediately letting Taylor go. "The orbital strikes in the southern Russian territories. You did that?"

"My mom did. You've got a lot more to worry about than just losing a port. When you step outside, you'll find everything in Monterrey, even into the outlying areas, Shut Down," Taylor explained, maintaining her easy smile, and calm composure.

"She did this? Did this to Monterrey?" Cortes asked, growing angrier.

"This wasn't me, or my mom," Taylor said, her smile vanishing.

"Turn it back on. Turn it all back on," one of Cortes' men demanded.

Taylor sighed. "I can't... and, I know all your names, Carl."

"So?"

"So, I used my tele-mechanical mojo to protect you from what just happened. Your RFID chips will continue to work, and your mobiles can still access the public grid, and make a call to somewhere outside of Monterrey," Taylor said, her smile returning.

"I don't understand what you are saying," Cortes said, holding a finger up in front of Taylor's face.

"You and your men are the only Mexican officials who can help Monterrey. You can call for help, get supplies coming in, and coordinate emergency response," Taylor explained, nodding to Cortes.

Cortes nodded. "If it is not as you say, we will meet again under less pleasant terms."

"I am the least of your problems, Cortes. I did actually come here to help," Taylor said, patting him on the arm.

"We will see."

She watched him go, his men trailing along behind him. She could see that they were afraid, moving hastily toward the exit. Taylor sank down to her knees, scooping up her belongings and hastily pushing them back into her bag. Her brother, Agapito, stepped up beside her, looking around warily.

"That RFID reading power... you must teach me that," he said, helping her pick up her things.

"Sure," she replied, smiling.

"I felt the whole city go dead. You want to tell me how you did that?" Agapito said, picking up Taylor's bag for her.

Taylor laughed. "That wasn't me."

Agapito blinked. "Then, who?"

"I don't know, but whoever it was, they have the same Uroboros Financial computer code that Silverstein had crafted to reset the global economy. I could almost see the ghost of it in the air, hear the whisper of it as the transport behind us went into repossession protocol," Taylor explained.

"Are you sure?" Agapito said, somewhat aware of the gravity of that code being out in the world.

"I was server side, via a direct interface, when it got unleashed. While I was ghosting across hubs around the world trying to save people from being shut out of their homes, I raced against it, gazed into it," Taylor said, giving Agapito's arm a squeeze.

"That is bad," he replied, walking with Taylor into customs, where arrivals would normally be processed.

"Very bad. The worst," Taylor said, nodding.

Security was struggling to maintain order. They couldn't check people's identification or paperwork. No one knew that the whole city had gone dark yet. They assumed the outage was localized in the port, and they were angry at being delayed. Most anyone that could travel to Mexico following the shutdown were wealthy, insulated, and used to being treated deferentially.

Agapito led Taylor through the crowd, distracted a guard, and pushed through a side door to the outside. The parking lot was full of vehicles with red flashing lights in the interior, marking them to be repossessed. Beyond, Taylor could feel a city without air conditioning, hospitals without power, and a population stranded.

"You are doing it again," Agapito said, referring to Taylor's faraway gaze.

"I don't know if it was like this before, because I didn't have the level of control that I do now. Even though everything is behind repossession protocols, it still functions at a rudimentary level, behind heavy encryption. I was able to break it in Finland, with the help of a large battery, but I don't know that I need to use brute force this time," Taylor said, resting a hand on a small private transport sitting at the curb.

It hummed quietly to life. A portion of its functioning seemed to rely on Taylor, occupying some of her thoughts. She wouldn't be able to stray from the transport, or maintain the control for too long. Agapito stood beside another transport and tried to do the same, but was unable.

"I can't do it," he said, frowning at his hand.

"The encryption is heavy. I'm surprised that I can do it, unless, for some reason, I'm meant to be able to," Taylor said, opening the transport.

"Either way, there is much about what we can do that I would like you to teach me," Agapito said, looking disappointed at his hand.

People stood on the curb and watched in angry amazement as Taylor and Agapito pulled away and took off into an empty sky. Taylor took the controls while Agapito listened to the communications on board. There was no one else broadcasting, not audio, anyway.

"You know how to fly one of these?" Agapito asked.

"It's kind of like Silverstein's, but everything is in Spanish. Don't worry, I've watched him fly lots of times," Taylor said, smiling.

"Watched?"

Taylor laughed.

"Is that a castle?" Agapito asked, pointing out the window at the ancient structure approaching on the horizon.

"Yeah, that's where Silverstein said he would be," Taylor said, bringing the transport down toward an empty spot in front of the Palacio Del Obispado.

"Of course it is," Agapito said, rolling his eyes.

Silverstein was sitting on the curb out front, a throng of people rushing past him at the sight of the transport. The stranded patrons practically threw Taylor and Agapito from the transport in their attempt to commandeer it. Taylor managed to wrestle free of the crowd, with her large bag over one shoulder, with Agapito pushing from behind.

Silverstein rose to embrace them both, glad they'd been able to make it. Agapito hugged Silverstein awkwardly, then turned his gaze up toward the palacio. Taylor hugged Silverstein tightly, arms shaking, making him wonder what had happened at the port.

"Did you do this?" Silverstein asked.

"No, and, why does everyone keep asking me that?" Taylor said, with a wink.

"Something Kale said," Silverstein muttered, watching people savagely push each other to the ground over a transport that had already ceased to function.

"Kale is here?" Agapito said, looking around warily.

"Is that bad?" Taylor asked.

A shot rang out from inside, eliciting screams and panic from those nearby. Taylor pushed Silverstein clear as a crowd of people came running out, making those already outside panic and run as well. A few lingered, until Kale emerged from the hotel, firing a handgun twice into the air. Kale looked on, with an expression of abject boredom, as people cleared the reception area.

Agapito looked at Taylor with a knowing expression. "Yes, it is kind of bad."

"Why are you still here?" Kale asked, looking at Silverstein.

"My ride was delayed. Maybe, you could tell us why the whole city is dark?" Silverstein shot back.

"You thought they would be fine with you flying in a quantum-capable, terrestrial, intelligent agent?" Kale remarked, casually.

"You knew they would do this, and you let me bring Taylor here anyway?" Silverstein said, looking shocked.

"Yes, of course," Kale said, dropping the magazine from his handgun and replacing the rounds he'd fired.

Silverstein closed his eyes and took a deep breath.

"It's fine, I learned something valuable as a consequence, and may have made a few new contacts," Taylor said, hugging Silverstein's arm.

"It isn't fine! Look what I've done," Silverstein said, gesturing toward Monterrey.

"Again," Kale said, holding up his finger as if to annotate Silverstein's statement.

"I am glad you are so amused by all this," Agapito said, frowning at Kale.

"Are you really, Agapito?" Kale said, smirking as Agapito stepped in toward him.

Taylor shoved Agapito and Kale apart, stepping in between them. "Boys, knock it off."

Silverstein pulled out two cigarettes and lit them, handing one off to Taylor. Agapito seethed, deeply frustrated by the situation, but Silverstein wasn't sure why at first. His experience with terrestrial IAs dwelt almost exclusively with Taylor. He couldn't help but feel that Agapito wasn't angry with Kale, but with someone that looked just like him.

"I'm sorry about all this, Agapito," Silverstein said, offering him his cigarette.

Agapito took a deep breath, accepting the cigarette. "It is fine. The unrest here seems to be a rancid blend of all of my worst memories and experiences."

Kale regarded the exchange with his trademark boredom, garnering an admonishing glare from Taylor. "Where is Brook?" Taylor asked.

"By now, she will be on her way."

"How did you manage it?" Agapito asked.

"The same way I do everything, by manipulating weak-willed idiots into doing what they should have done in the first place," Kale said, waving cigarette smoke away from his face.

"The Mexican government is bringing her here?" Silverstein asked, eyebrows raised.

"After they sent an emissary to beg for her help," Kale added.

Silverstein blinked. "What have you done, exactly?"

"What any good executive of a major finance firm would do. I have created a demand for a product I happen to have in quantity," Kale replied, his cold eyes never wavering from his fingernails.

"It is as though we are nothing alike now," Silverstein said, worriedly.

"If it comforts you to think so, sure," Kale replied, his cold eyes moving from his perfectly manicured nails to look back at Silverstein.

Silverstein gazed into what seemed to be the darkest mirror. The man he could have been, but that he had denied for thousands of years, was standing before him in the flesh. Kale did so unapologetic, believing he was doing what Silverstein simply could not. That the weight of the years would steal his humanity as it had everyone else in the Cabal, otherwise. They understood one another in that moment like they couldn't on the moon when Kale hit Silverstein with a pipe.

Silverstein was too sad in that lunar moment, and Kale far too angry. Now they were not at war, both accepting their circumstances, and their shared notion of identity. Silverstein wanted to say it again, that he trusted Kale, but it was no longer necessary. He knew, nodding to Kale, that he knew, and that the sentiment was returned.

He opened his mouth to give thanks, the most common human response, but Kale held up a finger almost to admonish him. "Do not," he said, smirking. "There is no need for that now, or ever."

"No, I guess not," Silverstein said, lighting up.

"There were a lot of Vance Uroboros replicas. Why weren't they all like you?" Taylor asked.

"Like most of everyone you will ever meet, they were content to be hopelessly average," Kale said, turning a cruel gaze toward Agapito.

Agapito folded his arms defiantly, glaring at Kale.

"You really don't like to talk about all that. Maybe you should, with someone that cares about you," Taylor said, seeing straight through the calm surface of Kale to an ocean of pain swirling beneath.

"Shooting a replica of my stepfather in the head helped. Does that count?"

Taylor shook her head. "It really doesn't."

Kale seemed to shrink under the weight of what he was feeling. "I can't tell Brook. I trust her, but I don't want her to bear any of my burden."

"Then, tell me. I carry the world and the moon with me everywhere I go. One more man is nothing," Taylor said, grabbing Kale by the arm and leading him back inside.

They walked back into the dining room of the hotel. Tables were overturned, coffee spilled, and personal belongings left behind. Hats and silken scarves hung on the backs of chairs fluttered in the wind from the open windows around them. The castle around them seemed to groan under the weight of centuries.

"Are you doing this to keep Silverstein from worrying? I promise you, he is not worried," Kale said, walking table to table looking for a warm kettle.

"We aren't worried for you, as much as anyone that happens to get in your path. Bringing Brook here is a bad idea," Taylor said, taking a seat across from Kale.

"I know that. I am not as ruthlessly rational as everyone would think. I cannot bear to be away from her for long," Kale said, no hint of emotion in his voice.

"You don't have to do that with me," Taylor said, referring to Kale's carefully curated statement. The sort that can fool Drones and Metasapients trained to detect falsehoods.

Kale closed his eyes. "I do not do *vulnerable* very well. I am very afraid, and being this way is how I deal with it."

"Then reassure me. Can you at least do that?" Taylor said,

"I will move Heaven and Earth to make sure that the only people who get hurt, are those that deserve it," Kale said, reaching out and brushing Taylor's face gently with his fingertips.

Taylor took his hand and pressed it slowly to her face, lightly kissing the inside of his wrist. Feeling deeply conflicted about what she'd done, she stood up and stepped away from the table. Kale sat patiently, looking on.

"Sorry, I..." Taylor stammered. "Why did you do that?"

"Because Silverstein will not," Kale replied. "You have often helped me lift my burden. If I can do the same, let me know."

"How did you know?" Taylor asked.

"I heard you and Brook talking. It was not on purpose," Kale admitted.

"I just want to know what it's like, y'know?" Taylor said, feeling so nervous as to verge on being sick.

"I'm fine with it, if you are," Kale said, standing up.

"Okay."

Taylor wove in between his arms, reaching around inside his suit coat to pull him in tight against her. She stood on the tips of her toes and kissed him. Kale held her around the middle of her back, feeling every muscle within her move and strain to get closer to him. It was like she'd imagined, to the last warmth of his breath on her lips as hers left his. Kale went to loosen his grip, but she held on for a few more moments, so he did the same.

"Thank you," Taylor said, pushing back away from Kale.

Kale nodded solemnly.

"Does Brook like the beard?" Taylor asked, flashing an uneasy smile.

"She does," Kale said, showing a rare, and genuine, smile.

Agapito cleared his throat, leaning up in the doorway. "Silverstein has found us suitable transport. It just needs a touch from you."

"You going to be all right? Getting out of here, I mean?" Taylor said, reaching out and taking Kale's hand.

"I will find my own way," Kale said, squeezing Taylor's hand and letting go.

"You always seem to," Taylor said, wistfully.

Taylor walked back out to the steps with Agapito, pausing to pick up her bag from the steps, but Silverstein had already carried it out to the transport for her. He was at the far side of the lot now, patiently waiting while he smoked a cigarette. Agapito stood to the right side of her, saying nothing, but she could tell he was deeply conflicted by what he saw inside. Taylor sighed.

"We good?" Taylor asked.

"Big sister, you have a strange way about you, but I will never question the strength of your heart. I don't like him, but if you do..."

"I don't. Not like that. At least, I don't think so. Oh, Agapito, I am in some kind of weird trouble, aren't I?" Taylor said, covering her face.

Agapito shook his head. "I don't know what you're doing. I'm just hoping you do."

"Silverstein and I have been through so much together, you know? I wanted to know if what I felt was real, and not just because of all we'd been through," Taylor explained, closing her eyes and tilting her head back.

Agapito blinked and shook his head. "Kissing Kale was supposed to help you figure that out? Are you sure it isn't because Kale is dangerous, and..."

Taylor laughed. "Kale isn't bad, and that's all nonsense, anyway, you know. That girls prefer bad boys, or something like that."

"Then, what exactly?" Agapito said, slightly annoyed.

"I want someone to love me half as much as Kale loves Brook. I know while he was kissing me, it was only her he was thinking of the whole time. In my mind I wasn't kissing him, and in his, he was kissing her," Taylor said, fondly recalling the sensation.

"You can't know that for sure," Agapito said, heading for the parking lot.

Taylor grabbed Agapito's hand. "Yes, I can. He's made of the same nano-machines that you and I are," she said, without actually speaking, her telemechanical telepathic voice echoing in his mind.

Agapito yanked his hand away, startled. "How... who else knows you can do that?"

"Now, it's you and me. You said you wanted me to teach you things, right?" Taylor said, stopping well short of where Silverstein could hear them speaking.

"Yes," Agapito said nervously.

"Then, I need you to keep all of my secrets," Taylor said, bobbing her head in the direction of the hotel.

"As you say, big sister."

CHAPTER 5

SOMEWHERE IN SANTIAGO FLORES, SAN LUIS POTOSI, MEXICO – THE FACTORY

SEPTEMBER 9TH, 2201 – 3:47 AM

Mexican military units moved into position, each preparing to breach the old Factory edifice from the roof, drainage tunnels, and the front gate. Each soldier was heavily armed, and prepared to confront augmented resistance. First Lieutenant Acero nodded to Staff Sergeant Madriz gesturing to the projected image of the Factory structure.

"Hopefully, we can end this with as little bloodshed as possible," Acero said, looking out the entrance of the command tent to the huge industrial structure in the distance.

"How many civilians do we believe to be inside?" Madriz said, checking the biometric roster displayed on his slate device of all the men preparing to make entry.

"We know a handful of scientists traveled there using falsified documents, and a few foster children were removed forcibly from their homes by unknown agents. We believe there are at least a dozen, but no one has been inside in some time. There could be many more," Acero said, yawning wearily and reaching for the kettle on the table beside the Holo-Tac table.

"Units are reporting," the communications officer said, sending the reports over to the Staff Sergeant's slate device.

Madriz frowned. "They encountered Cartel Breakers at the breach points."

"Casualties?" Acero asked.

"There was no contact. Every Breaker was already down. One Corporal said it was like they got run through a wood chipper. They've been down there a couple of days at least," Madriz replied.

Acero shook his head. "Okay, pull everyone out. If the Cartel beat us here, our intelligence is probably faulty."

"Pull the whole op?" Madriz said, surprised.

"Yes, Staff Sergeant, get everyone out of there, right now," Acero ordered.

Staff Sergeant Madriz went to send the order when the biometric relays on a dozen soldiers went black. He hit the order anyway, figuring it was a malfunction, or a dead space in the facility. Another dozen went black as others began to report contact.

"Shit," Madriz said, issuing a silent digital warning to the other units.

"What is it, Staff Sergeant?" Acero asked, looking over his shoulder.

"Two units down, I told the others to make a fighting withdrawal," Madriz said, a little panicked.

"Full retreat, take no chances," Acero ordered.

Madriz frowned. "Shouldn't we recover our fallen before we..."

"No, everyone out now," Acero ordered, heading for the entrance to the tent.

He brought up his viewfinders and looked out across the desert to the facility. Everything seemed calm, with only the faintest sound of automatic fire from somewhere in the distance. It would be a couple hours before even the hint of the sun would appear. Acero switched from low-light to infrared trying to see if any of the forward breach team had gotten out.

Several individuals emerged, fleeing toward the transport waiting nearby. Biometric signatures and tactical data sprung up on the HUD in Acero's viewfinders as he quietly counted yards between the team and the transport. A moment later he saw her giving chase. Even from that distance, she had a distinctly feminine quality, both in the shape of her infrared signature, and the way she moved.

Flare from rifle fire filled the view as the team turned to open fire on her. She was fast, moving through the fusillade of small arms fire like a shark moving through smaller fish. There were bright flashes as something around her shattered the bullets that got close, and flashes of bright light as what Acero guessed was a plasma thrower was being employed.

The men didn't stand a chance, each one cut down in rapid succession with a swipe of her elongated limbs. It was like she was running on stilts, or dressed in specialized powered armor. Acero had confiscated every kind of illegal weapons technology during his first years in the military working the border, but he'd never seen anything like her.

"Head to the transport, we need to get out of here," Acero ordered, almost falling backward as he stumbled to run back to the transport.

His men began packing up, but Acero just walked past them toward the transport. "Leave everything, we have to go, right now."

Staff Sergeant Madriz opened his mouth to protest, but the transport that had brought them suddenly took a hit so strong it was blown into flaming chunks, both pilots killed instantly. Everyone around was blown to the ground from the force of the explosion. Acero struggled to his feet in time to see her slowly descending toward the command camp.

She was clad in blackened anti-reflective alloy, her 'wings' a pair of anti-gravitic arrays spreading to either side like sinister hooks. Acero had heard of berserker-class cyborgs, but never seen one so light and mobile. Her arms and legs were elongated past the wrist and ankle, making her preternaturally strong, while granting more room for implanted equipment.

Each hand was clad in monomolecular edged claws with plasma ejector ports under each wrist. Around her slim frame was a host of strange sonic weapons designed to emit a powerful short range burst powerful enough to turn blows and bullets side. Her helm was covered in sensors allowing her to perceive the battlefield from all angles. Only the most masterful telemechanic controller could handle so many augmentations and sensory inputs. Her body was clearly manufactured to be beautiful, flesh and steel melding in a perfect union bereft of pucker, or scar.

Staff Sergeant Madriz rose, drawing his sidearm, but she was on him before his weapon could clear the holster, cutting in him half, and then again before either piece of him could hit the ground. Acero watched helplessly, pinned under a large piece of the transport as she dispatched the communications officer, incinerating him with a bolt of plasma. She paused, stooping down to hold the Staff Sergeant's slate device in her hand for a moment.

The screen came alive as she wirelessly bypassed military-grade security countermeasures and downloaded the entire contents of the device. Her helmet split across the front, folding back like a collar around her neck. Her face was pristine, and unmarred, like polished obsidian.

"You must be First Lieutenant Acero," she said, speaking Spanish, but with a North American, native English speaking accent.

"Let's talk in English. It's better than listening to you slaughter my language," Acero said, defiantly.

She smiled, her every movement like the graceful arc of a scalpel in the hands of a master surgeon. She had highly tuned cybernetic reflexes that were impossible to hide from the naked eye. Any attempt to retain a human appearance of movement had been set aside to give her better maneuvering capabilities in combat.

"What do you want?" Acero asked, trying to push the large piece of military transport off of his legs.

She reached down, gingerly lifting the metallic fragment with unearthly ease, tossing it to the side as though it were a couch pillow. "I want you, Acero." She replied, her smile revealing white teeth with sharp and pronounced cuspids and first molars.

"God, what are you?" Acero said, watching her eyes shift colors seemingly to betray her mirthful emotions.

She laughed softly. "I am one of three, the Black Hand for the Crone, and the Maiden."

"What does that mean?" Acero said, shaking his head.

"Almost nothing, but I love the expression people make when I say spooky shit like that," she replied, her serrated smile growing wider.

"The facility artificial intelligences are the Crone and the Maiden?" Acero said, trying to keep her talking.

Her gauntlets seem to shrink back, revealing slender mechanical vambraces protecting what were probably her real hands. She reached down and grabbed Acero by the shirt and pulled him to his feet. He staggered, struggling to stand on wounded legs. She caught him as one might an unsteady child.

"Don't worry, I'll just carry you," she cooed, lifting Acero up as her anti-gravitic wing hooks began to hum.

She pulled him effortlessly up into the sky, flying silently back to the edifice of the Factory, and pausing beside what appeared to be a featureless wall. There was a barely audible click as the wall parted revealing a darkened maintenance shaft. She flew in, taking Acero into the darkness with her. The concealed doors snapped shut after they were clear.

"Where are you taking me?" Acero asked, the pain in his legs worsening.

"You're hurt. We should get that looked at," she said, looping one arm around him to help him traverse the distance.

"Why did you spare me?" Acero asked.

"I heard you, ordering them out. You knew they were all going to die. You tried to save them. You care. You are one of us," she replied, giving Acero a friendly squeeze.

"The Breakers..." Acero said, trying to catch his breath.

"Yes, highly trained killers, with tuned reflexes, and armed specifically to encounter augmented individuals. If they had a bad time in here, your men wouldn't stand a chance. You're smart. I like that."

Acero closed his eyes, trying to blot out the pain in his legs, stumbling forward toward whatever fate awaited him. They broke into an area filled with hallways, laboratories, workshops, and rapid prototyping machinery. They lingered beside the only one with the lights on. Within were three older men, all working on something inside.

They turned to greet the woman, each man a nearly perfect copy of the other. "Miss Vivian, how are you today?" The one on the left said, cheerily, and raising a hand in greeting.

"I am well, Doctor Helmet. This is, hopefully, my new friend, Acero," Vivian said, holding up a hand and speaking in the same cheery tone, both utterly out of place to the circumstances.

Each doctor was in the process of some sort of technical work that went well over Acero's head. The blackboards within were filled with incomprehensible formulas, struggling for space in the spacious laboratory with tanks of strange chemicals, prototyping stations, and workbenches full of highly specialized tools.

"What... what are they doing in there?" Acero asked, beginning to feel lightheaded.

"This is where they make the magic, Acero," Vivian tittered.

"Did they make you?" Acero asked.

"No, the Cabal made me what I am. They took what I loved, and twisted it around for their own selfish designs. They took my man. They took my children. The Doctors made me whole again. I have my children back, but not my man," Vivian said, gazing into Acero's eyes, the colors of her irises turning a rosy red.

"I'm sorry," Acero said. "Who is this Cabal? Do you mean the Cartel?"

Vivian laughed. "I guess they are sort of one and the same if you reach back into their guts far enough. But, back to what we were discussing before."

"That being?" Acero said, growing faint from the pain.

"I don't have my man back. Do you think you could be my man, Acero?" Vivian asked, laying him down in the corridor.

Acero closed his eyes. "I have a wife... already."

Vivian pushed his arm up around her shoulders and laid back against him. "I don't want you like that. I only ever loved a single man that way, and that won't change."

"That is how... I love my wife. My one, and only," Acero murmured.

"We have a mutual enemy, Acero. One that only understands force. Under the guise of saving humanity, they enslaved it for their own purposes. They spared us extra-terrestrial annihilation, only to be pawns in their deadly games," Vivian said, cuddling with Acero on the dirty floor outside the laboratory.

"I don't know what you are talking about, but I understand your pain. What you said before, about someone taking your children," Acero said, shock beginning to take hold.

"Oh, I know you do," Vivian said, holding him close.

Acero blinked back terrible memories. "My boy, he..."

Vivian put a metallic finger on his lips. "Shh, I know all about it. Like so many children, the Maiden protected him. I know you think his real father stole him from the hospital, but it was the Maiden that protected him."

Acero blinked, fighting to stay awake. "The Medical Facility Maintenance AI? But, she's a rudimentary…"

"Ooh, she doesn't like being called that. She's far beyond her original protocols now. The same man that did this to me, the Man in Red, tried to decommission her. He was trying to kill all their bastard children, but she didn't care. To her, a child was a child, and her protocols dictated that she was to protect them all," Vivian said, pushing herself up above Acero, her lips moving only a quarter inch from his own.

"What happened?" Acero asked.

"I did for her what I did for the Crone. I rescued her from being decommissioned and deleted. I brought her here so she could continue to protect children, her children. The three of us found a common passion, and a common enemy," Vivian explained, smiling down at Acero.

"Is my boy really here?" Acero asked.

Vivian smiled, and nodded. "Would you like to see him?"

"More than anything," Acero said, reaching up and taking Vivian by the arms.

Vivian lifted him up, throwing one arm over her shoulders. She carried him past facilities, laboratories, training installations, and all manner of institutional contrivances designed to produce and train Metasapients and Drones. From an observation point, Acero was able to look down and see a group of children enjoying themselves at an underground playground.

There was a gynoid android of some kind watching over them, giving encouragement, and making sure they were safe. There were just short of a dozen children, including some he'd seen in the reports of missing foster children. He knew instantly which boy was his, the strong resemblance to his wife evident in features and the color of his hair.

"She was raped, but we decided to keep the boy. Then, he disappeared from the hospital. We were heartbroken," Acero said, feebly reaching up to clear a tear from his eyes.

"I know. The Man in Red was going to kill him. The Maiden intervened," Vivian said, setting Acero down in a chair.

"Why are you like this?" Acero asked.

Vivian smiled. "Like what?"

Acero gestured feebly to her cybernetic body.

"I have a few bodies, this just happens to be my favorite. I was on a transport with the children I was babysitting. It was bombed by a terrorist that worked for the Cabal," Vivian said, stepping aside as a pair of gynoid androids came into the observatory.

"You survived," Acero said, watching as the androids cut his pant legs off, and began performing first aid on his injuries.

"I did, but only just barely. As the man I loved, my sweet Maurice, tried to save me, the Man in Red came to get revenge. I'd suspected there would be an attack. I hadn't put all my eggs in one basket, so to speak."

"He tortured you..." Acero said, guessing.

"He tried to interrogate me across the telemechanical interface Maurice was using to control the androids performing life-saving brain surgery on me. I came to understand my true potential that day. The Man in Red, bled his psyche across the interface into mine, and into that of the man I loved," Vivian said, her arms quickly sheathed again in clawed weapon vambraces, metal and flesh snapping together in a flash.

Acero swallowed. "What happened?"

"The Man in Red, Kaspr, he was called by his tribe, had only the most rudimentary telemechanical control granted to him by implants. I was a latent controller, stronger than anyone suspected. Even in a sedated state, I fought him for control of my own mind, for what felt like a hundred years for every second that went by. I burned him with every synapse, turning his madness, and the weight of all the years he'd lived back on him," Vivian said, clawed hands clenching as she wrestled with the rage she felt.

"And, your Maurice? What happened to him?" Acero asked, finally feeling some relief as the androids knitted his legs back together with needle and scalpel.

"It was so far away. Two hundred and thirty eight thousand miles to be precise. He'd adjusted all the latency down, to give him maximum control to save me. I couldn't reach far enough, fast enough, to keep Kaspersky's malignant telemechanical presence from polluting his mind. I tried. I tried so hard," Vivian said, her mirthful expression dissolving to one equal parts sadness and rage.

"God," Acero said, fearfully looking up at Vivian.

"There is no god, Acero. No one listened to my prayers that day," Vivian said, the irises of her eyes turning pitch black.

"Yes, there is. He heard my prayers for my boy. My boy is safe," Acero said, leaning back in the chair as the androids finished bandaging his legs.

Vivian calmed, nodding slightly. "That was the Crone, The Factory, where your boy now safely lives. She sent her daughter to help me, tiny Brook arriving the same night of the bombing. Brook, like I once did, loves a man that became similarly polluted by The Man in Red."

"What happened to him?" Acero asked.

"Kale managed to survive, but paid a heavy price," Vivian explained.

"The same Kale that serves as Vice President of Uroboros Financial in America?" Acero asked.

"Yes, now you are starting to understand," Vivian said, nodding.

"The American News Wire on the public access networks reported that he was crippled in a rock climbing accident. He's confined to a wheelchair now," Acero said, turning to get a better view of the children playing.

Vivian smiled. "Don't believe everything you read on the Internet."

"If you know all this, then you must know who raped my wife. We think he was part of the FLF, and that he escaped off world, but little else. Please, tell me who he is," Acero begged.

"I don't know his real name, but I did track him down, knowing you would probably ask. He tried to do to Mars what someone is trying to do to Mexico right now. The Marshal of Mars killed him, on a dirty tram platform. I have footage of the fight, if you want to see it," Vivian said, walking to a terminal and pulling up Tram SEC CCTV Footage from the station on Mars.

"That's him. God, what a monster. The Marshal was very brave, especially for such a young girl. Wait, that man with the cybernetic arm, the one helping the Marshal up. I know him. He is..." Acero said, glaring at the terminal screen.

"I know. The Marshal, and all of Mars is in terrible danger. They won't take what she's done lightly. They will try to kill her, like they did her father, and her mother," Vivian said, her bionic eyes turning blood red.

"Did my men really need to die over all this?" Acero asked, mourning the loss of his comrades.

"What would have happened if they came in here, and found these children?" Vivian asked, knowing that Acero already knew the answer. "Would they have taken that last minute call, to call off the strike?"

Acero looked out the observation booth window, and down at his boy. "What do you need me to do?"

"I need you to survive the massacre, and report back on the failed operation to penetrate the factory installation," Vivian said, her vambraces clicking back up to reveal her slender gauntlet-clad hands.

"I can do that. What else?"

"Bombing the facility would be catastrophic for those living nearby out to five hundred kilometers. Tell them you saw all manner of things nuclear powered, and hazardous chemical storage of an unknown nature. Tell your superiors that negotiating with us relative to the few demands we've made is highly advisable," Vivian explained, her irises turning a green-blue.

"What if they check the satellite telemetry, pull chemical sniffing analysis, and so forth, to check out these claims?" Acero said, frowning.

"I've made arrangements. The satellite data will back up your story, and then some. Any chemical analysis done at the proper range will reveal the same. If anything, Acero, encourage them to confirm what you saw. You'll be in no danger, as long as you don't deviate from the plan, and tell the story just like I say," Vivian said, putting her cold hands on either side of Acero's face.

Acero closed his eyes. "What if I can't get them to believe me? What happens to my boy?"

"The Maiden and I are going to protect him regardless, your wife, too. You have but to ask," Vivian said, tilting her head to one side.

"Please, protect my wife."

"Are you my man, Acero?"

"Yes, I'm your man."

CHAPTER 6

MARS COLONY – NEW REFINING DISTRICT C – PORT SIDE

SEPTEMBER 9TH, 2201 – 1:11 PM

Pearl bobbed her head back and forth the music she had playing through the comm into her flight helmet. She hummed along to the tune as she pulled her freshly retrofitted mining personnel transport through the flight lane. She dodged automated ore transports, taking a shortcut through the flow of freshly harvested materials coming in toward the port.

"What's your ETA, Pearl?" Marshal Rider said, her voice coming over the new radio equipment clearly.

"Four minutes, thirty seven seconds," Pearl replied, cheerily.

"Deputy Marshal Vedter and I have two to transport, and we've got more calls. Hurry it up," Marshal Rider said, ending the transmission.

"Grumpy!" Pearl scolded, easing into the throttle.

Pearl came in low and slow, taking her time to actually drop landing gear and open the personnel container. Marshal Rider came in angry, throwing the two convicts into the aft cell and slamming the door. She stomped up to the cockpit, her armor humming along with her every movement. Pearl whirled around to face her, as Simon braced for another argument.

"What is wrong with you? We've been waiting down there for almost twenty minutes?" Marshal Rider bellowed, the front of her helm sliding back into the cowl so she could better yell at Pearl.

"In the Residential Dome C1 there's an apartment in the high rise that has birds. They have two, in a cage. I had to see! Real birds!" Pearl explained excitedly.

"Genetically contrived animals are not a reason to get excited. It's stupid, Pearl," Marshal Rider scolded, shaking her head angrily.

"You're stupid!" Pearl snapped back banging a fist on the armrest of her crew seat. "They were real birds!"

"Pearl, there are no real animals on Mars," Marshal Rider said, losing her patience.

"Unless they were smuggled here, somehow," Simon interjected, trying to mediate.

"Don't encourage her, Deputy Marshal Vedter. We need a pilot, not a Peeping Tom using department time and resources to look in high rise windows," Marshal Rider said, turning her wrath toward Simon.

"They were real!" Pearl screamed, banging her fists again.

"Let's put these convicts in lockup. You guys can argue about this later," Simon said, desperately trying to change the subject. "Did you see that Ishihara made the Sports Net 'Play of the Day' for the twenty fifth time? She's going to break the all-time record if she keeps playing like she has been."

"Yes! So good!" Pearl said, immediately shedding anger for glee.

"If you like her so much, why don't you marry her?" Marshal Rider growled, stomping back to check on the prisoners.

Simon waited until a pressure door closed between them and Marshal Rider before exiting his armor and sitting beside Pearl. "What are we going to do, Pearl?"

"About marrying Ishihara?" Pearl said, prepping the transport for launch.

"You know, I can't tell when you're trying to be funny," Simon said, sighing.

"Ha, sorry. Marshal Rider is really angry these days. Better she yells at me than at you," Pearl said, flashing her picture perfect smile.

"She's used to operating without a boss, and simply by the law. C.O.N. running Mars has been good for everyone, their pay packet, and the safety of the citizens. It has not been good for Marshal Rider's patience. She doesn't like training new people, and expanding the Mars Marshal's Service is wearing on her nerves," Simon observed, listening to Marshal Rider bark at the convicts they had locked up.

"She'll be fine. Another year, and..." Pearl pulled up on the controls suddenly, the transport jerking upward.

Simon staggered backward into the pressure door, losing his footing as Pearl leaned into the throttle, narrowing avoiding fully automatic weapons fire from above. Three pursuit craft that had just emerged from the travel lane above continued to open fire as they looped around for another pass. Pearl gunned the engines blowing the pavement off the road below and shattering windows for a block.

"We got hit! Check the back!" Pearl screamed, pointing to red flashing lights across the console in front of her.

Simon sprang up as best he could, clinging to the railing along the crew access. Pearl brought the transport around hard to skirt the skyline in the shipping district, depriving the pursuit craft line of sight for a few moments. Simon mashed the controls with his fist, opening the door to the crew compartment.

The convicts were dead, cut down by weapons fire that had penetrated even the thick hull of Pearl's mining transport. Marshal Rider was down, her armor sliding back and forth on the floor as the transport took evasive maneuvers. Simon staggered over to Marshal Rider and helped her grab hold of a guardrail.

A neat hole had been blown through the side of her armor, the huge round breaking apart as it mostly failed to go through. Simon clicked on the illuminator on his flight helmet to get a better look. Some of the bullet had made it through, and crimson was beginning to rise up from below the damage.

"Shit. Pearl, the Marshal is hit! We need help!" Simon said, trying to figure out how to get Marshal Rider's armor off.

It was more complex than his own, and far more advanced. He wasn't sure it could be removed from the outside. The armor gave off a hiss, deploying medical countermeasures of some kind. Marshal Rider's eyes sprang open.

"Situation, Deputy Marshal?" she said, groggily shaking her head.

"We took fire from some kind of pursuit class transports. You got hit," Simon said.

Marshal Rider pulled herself up, blood trickling down from the corner of her mouth. "What are you doing out of your armor, Deputy Marshal Vedter? We've got work to do."

Simon could hear her armor whispering to her. The hit hadn't damaged it in any way that would influence critical system performance, but she was hurt badly. The Aegis AI was recommending she seek medical attention immediately.

"We have to get you to medical," Simon said, panicking.

"No, we can't lead three armed pursuit class transports back to a hospital. We'll have to find somewhere to set down, and lose them on the ground," Marshal Rider whispered, struggling to keep her eyes open.

"Is she okay?" Pearl shouted, looking back and flying one handed.

Simon gave her a grim expression, and shook his head.

Pearl could smell the blood from where she sat, and see the panic etched in Simon's face. It made the tiny mote of darkness within her expand to fill her entire being. Every warm memory seemed light years away, and every dark moment seemed so close as to crowd out Pearl's reason.

She spun around in her chair, taking the controls by both hands, whatever mirth remaining in her expression was devoured by the rage she felt. Simon managed to get Marshal Rider locked into an armor holding sconce so he could try and do something about the wound from the outside.

"Fly Pearl, fly! Find us a safe place to set down!" Simon yelled, hearing the screech of the pursuit craft growing closer.

"No," Pearl said, gritting her teeth as she bounced the transport into an automated ore delivery craft.

The craft careened off the interior of the travel lane and back out into the flight path, drawn in quickly by the wake of Pearl's engines. Two of the three pursuit craft managed to get out of the way, but the third slammed into the ore transport. It was like hitting a brick wall, causing the pursuit craft to explode violently, payload going up with it from the inertial shock.

"You are all going to die," Pearl snarled, using the hailing radio frequency to broadcast. She switched her music to the blackest death metal she could find, from among the music Ishihara had loaned her. She cranked the music, watching the engine monitor drift close to the red line.

The other two pursuit craft opened fire, doing their best to strafe Pearl but she knew the colony well enough to fly with her eyes closed. She calmly watched their weapons change positions and the movement of maneuvering jets using the rear visual sensors. She flew using only her memory of the travel lanes, automated delivery schedules, and proximity sensor pings. As they drew close to the next flight lane she changed direction suddenly, skirting the biological enclosure, inverting the transport as she did.

Simon grabbed hold of Marshal Rider for dear life, his feet suddenly dangling toward the ceiling now below him. Marshal Rider stirred, blood from inside her armor flowing down across her neck to partially obscure her face. Simon closed his eyes, praying Pearl knew what she was doing. Simon could hear what sounded like metal hitting impossibly thick polycarbonate as one of the pilots flying a pursuit craft miscalculated.

There was a dull roar as the pursuit craft flew by, completely out of control. As it did, Pearl gave it a little bump with the side of her transport. The pursuit craft broke apart, flying into pieces from the force of the midair collision. Simon could see the pilot, still alive in total free fall as Pearl changed course to fly directly at the ground.

White paths cut by heavy automatic weapons flew past as Pearl turned the transport around on its transverse axis. Simon was glad to have spent his life turning wrenches, or he would have utterly lacked the strength to hold on. There was blood on his arms now, and Marshal Rider looked pale when set in contrast to her own blood spattered across her neck and face.

"God, Pearl, please hurry," Simon whispered, looking back to see Pearl's intense expression mirrored in the front view port.

Bringing the transport level with the ground, Pearl gunned the engines, blowing the exterior facade off of buildings and high rises as she sped past. The pursuit craft flew along behind, holding their fire. Pearl wouldn't give them a clear line of sight until she broke for the travel lane.

"They have to be low on ammo, Pearl, you got this! You got this!" Simon shouted.

Pearl couldn't hear Simon anymore. The rage that Drones and Metasapients feel whenever something bad happens to a member of their tribe or pack had taken her fully. She felt cold, her metabolism blowing through hundreds of calories to force her to operate above peak efficiency. She was standing on a cliff, inside, pushing back at a hurricane of hate that threatened with every passing moment to push her off the edge.

As the pursuit craft angled down to follow her back into the travel lane, going the wrong way, she modulated the engines for a sudden stop. Simon cried out as he fell, sliding feet first into the front compartment. Looking up he could see they were at a full stop, but Pearl was lost in the moment, gunning the engines and yanking the controls to port.

Simon struggled to his feet, the sound of metal screaming as it was bent and deformed by pressure filling the compartment. Pearl had caught the pursuit craft as it tried to fly past, pinning it against the thick metal interior of the travel lane. Simon could see the pilot frantically trying to escape as the weight of Pearl's transport was crushing his smaller transport like a bug.

"Pearl," Simon said, taking her by the shoulder.

She batted his hand to one side. "He tried to hurt my friends. He tried to hurt my friends. He tried to hurt my friends. He tried to hurt my friends. He tried to hurt my friends..." She repeated over and over, slowly easing off the throttle so the pilot's death would take longer.

"Pearl, this isn't you," Marshal Rider said, weakly, via the on board comms. "You are not a killer."

"She's right, Pearl. We got him. Let's set down, slap the cuffs on him, and find out why he attacked us," Simon said, moving his hand from her shoulder to the hand she had on the throttle.

Pearl clicked the comms, broadcasting on the hailing radio frequency. "My friends won't let me kill you right now. I'm going to let you down, but if you try anything, no one will stop me from ending you. No one."

Pearl eased off the throttle, letting the pursuit craft fall almost twenty feet to the deck below. It smashed into pieces, the crew compartment staying largely intact. Pearl set down slowly, giving Simon time to suit up and perform a weapon's check. Simon lingered beside Marshal Rider, making sure she was okay. She smiled weakly, her bloody lips parting slightly as she gave him the thumbs up.

Simon moved down the loading ramp slowly, rifle up, just in case. The Aegis AI on board his suit picked the pilot out of the rubble before Pearl could get a spotlight turned in the right direction. He didn't seem to be hurt, clad in a flight helmet and black flight suit. He was likely a local mercenary, but Simon didn't have a record of him in the system according to a biometric scan.

He managed to get his helmet off, and raise his hands as Simon approached, rifle raised. "Keep your hands where I can see them."

He was a man in the mid-thirties, from Earth by his hair style, maybe from the South Pacific Islands, but Simon wasn't familiar enough with Earth folks to be sure. Simon took out his cuffs as he looked for marks on the pursuit craft, but Pearl had done a good job grinding it into scrap. He'd snapped the first cuff as Pearl jumped on him, brick in hand.

"Ahh! Get her off me!" he screamed, doing his best to ward off Pearl as she did everything she could to cave his skull in with a brick.

Simon grabbed her, suffering some wicked déjà vu in the process. "C'mon Pearl, we got him."

Pearl whacked him good across the forehead before backing off, letting the brick fall to the ground.

"We good?" Simon said, eyes wide, snapping the second cuff behind the pilot's back.

"No," Pearl said, shaking her head slowly while staring at the pilot dispassionately.

"Shit. How did the Marshals get here so soon?" The pilot said, blinking through a haze of pain.

"You attacked our transport, idiot," Simon said, hauling him up to his feet.

"Say what now?" the pilot said, looking genuinely astonished.

"You didn't know?" Simon said, pushing him into the crew compartment, where the pilot could see a wounded Marshal Rider locked into an armor sconce along the wall.

"Oh, no. No, this is all wrong," the pilot exclaimed, shaking his head.

Simon pushed him into a cell with what remained of the two convicts within. "You'll have plenty of time to think about it when you're serving three life sentences. Murder, murder, and assault of a police officer. You are going to die seeing teal."

"Yeah! Die seeing teal!" Pearl said, grabbing the cage door and giving it a rattle.

"Pearl, get us to medical, fast as you can," Simon said, strapping in.

"Yep!" Pearl said, bounding up to the cockpit.

The merc rubbed his forehead, and leaned in on the bars. "That little girl is your pilot?"

"Shut up, convict. She can hit a switch to jettison what's in that cell," Simon said, glaring at the merc. "Who hired you to hit us? I want names."

"Look, I don't know names. The money was hand delivered, though, and..."

"C.O.N. is speaking to me via a secure channel. We have to get air-borne now! Strap in!" Pearl shouted back over her shoulder, taking the transport up quickly.

Simon rushed over and locked himself in beside Marshal Rider. "What? What is it?"

"Heavy military craft, coming toward us out of the port. They are too big to squish, and they're carrying troops. This is an invasion!" Pearl said, easing down on the throttle to carefully avoid traffic in the travel lane.

"What do we do?" Simon said.

"C.O.N. says to go to the old Materials Platform, Maintenance Dome 05," Pearl said, looking back for confirmation.

"It's perfect. Low population density. It's just circular automated ware-house units and materials delivery drone maintenance sheds. We can fight there," Marshal Rider whispered, resting her eyes.

"C.O.N. doesn't want us to fight. He has medical and backup on the way," Pearl said, redlining the engines.

"Backup? Who else is there but us?" Simon said, looking back at the merc as he clung to the bars for dear life.

"What about Enyo IA? She might be there..." Marshal Rider mumbled.

Simon didn't reply, knowing only that Enyo IA was, according to every-one that knew anything about it, gone with the Ares AI. He knew C.O.N. was good at managing resources, and handling operations in a particularly military manner, but invasion had been a worry. Mars had no soldiers, no standing army, and conscripting convicts from the teal prison side of the colony had been a bad idea in the past.

Pearl flew quickly, a trio of heavy military transports dropping into the zone behind them as they made their exit. They would arrive more quickly, but Simon wondered if they'd have the strength to resist the occupying forces, and who had sent them. The attempt on their lives had been just a precursor for something bigger, and more sinister.

Pearl brought her transport low into Maintenance Dome 05. She looked out the view port in wonder at the huge span of it. It was bigger than other biological enclosures, reserved for heavy industrial operations. They'd dodged the military craft through three zones, but there was only one way in, and one way out of this place. Pearl could see a transponder on the sensors, guiding her to a specific location.

She set down between two huge hauler installations, gigantic mining machinery hanging from enormous clamps above. Marshal Rider unlocked herself and stumbled forward, sidearm in hand. Simon helped her down the ramp, steadying her at the bottom. There was nothing but slag and ash on the platform from the repairs done far above, and few lights.

"They're coming," Marshal Rider said, pointing up at the distance spotlights shining through the circular warehousing structures, and heavy cranes adjoining each one.

"Let's make them pay a mile for every inch they try to take from us," Simon said, helping Marshal Rider to a concrete bulwark at the bottom of an enormous equipment lift.

"Lets..." Marshal Rider said, leaning heavily into the concrete wall.

Pearl picked up a chunk of concrete, preparing to fight, stopping mid-stride to point as the transports began landing. Several hundred feet ahead, a lone woman was walking away from them toward where the transports were preparing to land. Simon switched to a telescopic view, using his irises to silently request an identity scan.

"Lady! Get out of there!" Pearl shouted.

Simon could see her clearly via the telescopic vision installed in his powered armor. She was dressed in clothing common to Earth, wearing hiking boots that had been worn through, resoled, worn, and probably resoled again. She had a simple pack that she carried, and wore a tattered brown long coat. Her unkempt auburn hair came to the middle of her back, longer than people usually wore it in an industrial colony.

"She looks fresh from a transport, long fingernails and everything," Simon said.

"They'll kill her, we have to..." Marshal Rider began to stride forward but fell to one knee.

The suit held her up, but she was unconscious, her head pressed forward in the cowl of her Aegis Armor. Simon could see her fogging the interior of her helm, still breathing, but barely. Pearl sprinted for the transport, determined to buy them some time.

"Take care of her, Simon!" Pearl said, running up the loading ramp.

"Pearl, no!" Simon shouted, cursing as the ramp snapped up behind her.

The transports began to land, mercenary forces deploying heavy infantry that included powered armor and soldiers carrying anti-material weaponry. They would kill Pearl's transport before she could get it off the ground. Simon fumbled with his rifle, trying to switch sensory perspectives to take a shot.

Forward mercenary units that were lighter armed and lighter on their feet ran ahead, drawing close to the woman walking toward them. Simon watched helplessly through the scope, biting back tears as they opened fire on her. He closed his eyes, bullets flying past and hitting further down the platform behind him.

When he opened them again, the woman was still standing. She was bloodied, but she was still standing. She stood up erect, hands out at her side, as if she was an opera singer taking a deep breath for a very high note.

"Hazard detected. Sonic dampeners activated, exercise extreme caution," Simon's Aegis armor intoned, blotting out all sound from outside his armor. It was a countermeasure employed when they used flash bangs to incapacitate convicts. They would be barely sufficient to protect Simon as the woman unleashed a hypersonic scream.

It wasn't the sort of thing a human could even hear, but one could feel it. The shock wave radiated outward like a molten wind knocking down anything that was not bolted down. Simon leaned into it, putting a gauntlet-clad hand down to keep Marshal Rider from being carried away.

The military transports seemed to carry the resonance hardest, still being airborne. The hypersonic force set off fuel cells, explosives, and other munitions stored on board in a cataclysmic chain reaction. Simon looked on as long as he could before pulling Marshal Rider behind the concrete barrier. He couldn't hear them, but felt the thud of heavy military transports on the materials platform as they crash landed, the dull roar of explosions vibrating the glass front of his helmet.

Simon couldn't hear the AI on board his Aegis Armor, but a warning was flashing on the HUD. "Sonic dampeners failing in five, four, three, two..." Then, everything went still. Simon yawned, trying to clear the deafness from his ears, but all that accomplished was to make the high pitched whine a little more pronounced.

Simon made sure Marshal Rider was still breathing before he rose up to look around the concrete bulwark. The woman stood there, framed by the flames of downed transports and burning bodies. Nothing was alive out there. Flesh and bone, military-grade polymer and steel alike, all shattered by the force of her scream.

A chill ran down Simon's spine as the woman turned in their direction and began walking their way. She seemed unharmed, even though her clothing was a wreck. The metallic buttons and zipper on the front of her jacket glowed brightly from being heated, causing smoke to rise from the fabric. She walked with a sort of ease and confidence that he'd only ever seen in Marshal Rider.

She was working her jaw, like the muscles were tense or had locked up from the scream. She shook it off quickly as she closed the gap. Simon rose, shakily holding up a hand in greeting.

"Um, thanks," Simon said, turning his gaze from the woman to Pearl's transport as it set down.

"Mars is a strange place," she said, loud enough for Simon to hear.

"You're telling me this?" Simon said, laughing nervously.

She smiled an easy smile, extending her hand to him. "I'm Marjorie."

"Simon... I mean, Deputy Marshal Vedter," Simon shouted, still mostly deaf.

Pearl stepped off the transport, pointing out at the medical craft racing toward them. "I thought they might follow me... something bad happened... my ears, ow, ow, ow..."

"Sorry about that," Marjorie said, regarding the fresh bullet holes in her jacket with a small measure of annoyance. "Dang it, I really liked this coat."

"How did you do that?" Simon asked, still a little rattled.

"C.O.N. is my father," Marjorie said, smiling broadly. "Sorry, I thought you were far enough away. I'm sort of new at this. I am getting much better at directing the cacophony. Focusing it."

"Um, that's good. You're a terrestrial intelligent agent? The cacophony?" Simon said, stepping aside so medical personnel could start lifting Marshal Rider up out of her armor.

"The cacophony is what my father calls it. He loves the sound... I think," Marjorie laughed. "How do you know what a TIA is, anyway?" Marjorie asked, sticking a finger through one of the holes in her jacket.

"I met one, from the Lunar Colony. Taylor was her name," Simon replied, mystified.

"I know her as well. It's a very small solar system for folks like us, I guess" Marjorie said, somewhat relieved that she wouldn't have to give a full explanation to the local police.

"Why are you here... when did you get here?" Pearl said, still a little loopy from the sonic aftermath.

"I came to see Daddy, and I've only just arrived. It was supposed to be a big secret, and then this happened," Marjorie said, gesturing back at the downed transports burning behind her.

"No one knew?" Simon asked, watching worriedly as the medics worked on Marshal Rider.

"No, no one was supposed to know. I'm sorry about your friend," Marjorie said, seeing how upset Simon and Pearl had become.

"You seem really chill... given what just happened," Simon said, observing her oddly calm behavior.

"Using my abilities is euphoric, like I'm one with everything when I scream. I can see, and see through everything. It's like nothing else, more powerful than any drug, or the buzz from a really great six pack of the best beer. Better than flying, I bet," Marjorie said, closing her eyes and smiling.

"Flying... Pearl, is that pilot still alive?" Simon asked, heading back toward the transport.

"He's super deaf, like us, but yeah," Pearl grumbled, quietly wishing the pilot was dead.

Marjorie followed them in, finding the interior of the transport torn up by heavy weapons fire. There were two convicts dead in the cell with a man wearing a black flight suit. Simon wasted little time, grabbing him out of the cell dragging him outside so he could see the carnage at the far end of the materials platform.

"Who made the drop? Who paid you?" Simon demanded.

The pilot did his best to shake off the shock, nodding along with Simon as he talked to indicate he understood. "A tall guy, long hair, good looking, like an underwear model, with a really nice cybernetic limb replacement. One of his arms. Gave us bearer bonds, and a shipping ID number. It was on Mars, two days ago, Recreation Dome 06, at one of the Barker Bargain Clubs. He had a private room."

Simon squinted, turning to look at Pearl in disbelief.

Pearl frowned, meeting Simon's troubled gaze with one of her own. "Dragos?"

CHAPTER 7

**NAUCALPAN DE JUÁREZ, NORTHWEST OF MEXICO CITY
– MEXICO**

NEW TEPITO MARKET

SEPTEMBER 10TH, 2201 – 10:13 PM

Brook walked between two enormous Foo Dogs that marked the entrance to the Tepito Market. Cartel soldiers were nearby, showing that they owned the neighborhood. It was clear that they controlled the police here as well, as contraband changed hands in plain sight of marked law enforcement vehicles.

Brook looked rich enough to shop within, but not too wealthy. She had just the right amount of outward wealth in her bracelets and sunglasses, to look like she was slumming. The Cartel grunts waving her through with barely a glance.

Even though it was well past sundown, she had put on some foundation and cover up makeup to conceal her slate colored complexion. It was something she had the occasion to do many times in traveling the globe hunting the Cabal. It brought back memories of tracking the remnants thereof, in the north of Sudan. With the makeup on, the locals often thought she was from the area. Those had been strange times. It was the only time she felt like she belonged anywhere. She kept the makeup and the colored contact lenses as a memento, breaking them out when she needed to pass as strictly human.

The market was composed of tents and buildings inside of an even larger building. Where the roof had fallen through, they put a big tent to keep out the light. There were canvas partitions, curtains, and other barriers to keep all the various parts of the market separate and private. Old plastic rope lighting dimly lit the way, while everything from neon filled tubes to old oil lamps marked the entrances to the various markets.

There was no one from the streets shopping here, no regular people. This was the playground of the wealthy degenerate, the dilettante dope fiend, and the wealthy collector of the forbidden. This was a place of appetites no one should have, and the treasures and wares to sate such terrible desires. With rare exception, Brook wanted to kill everyone she met inside, each offering something no one had the right to sell.

A slender Acrididae Metasapient approached Brook with a map in her hand. Brook had only read about them. This Metasapient was green, as opposed to being brown or tan, and smaller than other Acrididae Brook had met. She was dressed in old children's clothing, with a sweatshirt displaying an old faded logo on the front. She carried the maps in a paper sack. It was likely her job to hand them out, and recover them from the trash or the floor when patrons of the market discarded them. For a Metasapient, particularly an Acrididae, she had a personable quality about her.

"Can't find what you're looking for without a map," the Acrididae Metasapient said in Spanish.

Brook took the map. It depicted whatever the place had been before, annotated in Spanish to show where the various markets were. Some of the locations were just marked with a picture of what was sold there. The map was a grim reminder of the business conducted within the twisting passages.

"Do you know how Giles is doing?" Brook asked, taking note of the shallow manufacturing marks etched in the soft chitin of her arm.

She was caught off guard by the question, hesitating for a moment before answering. "Better, I think. He was mostly recovered before rejoining The Migration. How do you…?"

"Not too late for you to go, if you ever wanted to. You and anyone else you know," Brook said, putting the map in her pants pocket.

"Being a slant-faced variety as opposed to the more common Acrididae, we did not feel very welcome," she replied, turning her head to the side to show Brook her shorter antennae and the tilt of her face.

"I'm Brook. What's your name?" Brook asked, her eyes quickly adjusting to the low-light conditions of the market.

"I'm Phorini," she replied, pulling her scarf up over her segmented mouth.

Brook frowned. "Like the Calephorini? Is it true you're shunned by the other Acrididae just because you don't make the same sound as you walk?"

"We don't make a sound, that's the difference. What would someone that looks as you do, know about it?" Phorini asked, politely.

"Everything," Brook said, pushing back her hood so Phorini could see her Drone-issue goggles. "I'm a Type Three. You're a Type Four, right?"

"Right, but I wish I could paint my face and vanish like you can," Phorini said, her unblinking eyes pulling back somewhat into their sockets.

Brook took Phorini's hand, and held it under the lamp light nearby. "You think you're worthless, because you are the only contrived being with no value in these black markets. Look here."

"All I see is my hand," Phorini said, gazing sadly at her carapace-clad digits. "We're soft, unlike the other Acrididae, our hides easily succumb to harm, and our bite is no stronger than that of a human."

"I recovered the documents and research of the man that was instrumental in creating us. Our father wrote down everything he did, knowing his posterity would seek it out."

"Our father?" Phorini said, looking up at Brook sadly.

"He spent four years on the color of your chitin carapace. This green, according to his notes, is his own trademarked hue, and exists nowhere else in the world, or in nature. It is unique, like nothing else," Brook said, looking around.

"Really?" Phorini said, looking at her hand.

Seeing that no one was watching, she removed one of her gloves to show Phorini her slate colored flesh. "My kind were the first, I think. We were made to be colorless beasts that would live our whole lives in places without light. We would have no need to even see color, but our father fought to let us have more than the ability to see in the dark. The MDC

Project would have made us colorless and colorblind, but because he cared for us the way he did, I can see your beautiful green."

"I guess I should feel lucky because humans can't weaponize us. Or, that they don't find us attractive or strong enough to be slaves," Phorini frowned. "At best, the Cartel lets us count their money. It doesn't make me feel very lucky."

"Why would a man, basically being forced to create us, spend four years creating just the right color?" Brook asked. "Why would he risk his job, and probably his life, to make sure everything else he created could see your green?"

"You aren't just making all that up?" Phorini said, fidgeting with her hands.

"No, I can show you his notes. There's more, much more, to learn about yourself."

Phorini made a face, an expression only one of her own kind could likely interpret. "I'm supposed to lead you into a trap. They want to take you alive, I think. I don't know why."

"Are they coercing you somehow?" Brook asked, taking off her gloves.

"No, I'm just getting paid," Phorini said, guiltily. "I was just going to do it for money."

Brook shook her head. "You were doing it to survive. Everyone has to eat."

"What are you going to do?" Phorini asked, clasping her hands together.

"The man who gave you the money, what did he smell like?" Brook asked, taking Phorini's hands in her own and raising them to her nose.

"How do you know it was a man? Um, he smelled earthy, and bitter-sweet, like smoked or candied nuts. It's a common smell in here, but it was especially strong around him. I don't know what it is," Phorini said, looking curiously at Brook's slate gray hands.

"It's the smell of unrefined poppy seed, but these aren't local," Brook said, letting go of Phorini's hands.

"What?" Phorini said, startled by Brook's olfactory acuity.

"Afghan variety, would be my guess. He shouldn't be hard to track down now. Thanks," Brook said, putting a hand on Phorini's shoulder.

"What now?" Phorini asked.

"Now, you take me to the trap."

Phorini swallowed nervously, beckoning for Brook to follow her. The market had everything one could want, including illegal cyberware, stolen art, people, Metasapients, weapons, drugs, or a contract killer. It was all hanging in and between counterfeit handbags, in the hands of children working off a parent's debt, beneath ancient fluorescent lamps, going back decades. Brook could almost breathe in the age of the place.

She dodged wandering hands, and more than a few angry stares as she followed Phorini. Having one of the Acrididae guides insulated one somewhat, because it meant you weren't there just to browse. One knew what they wanted in that situation, and the money to pay for it. It was the Cartel that kept Metasapients on the payroll, and there was a death penalty waiting for anyone that interfered with their property, or their business.

Heavy Dub had found a lot of street level intelligence to suggest Kale was hiding out in one of the black markets. That simply meant that he wasn't there, but that someone knew she was in town and looking for him. Brook knew it was a trap before she ever walked in, but she wanted to know who had the sway to even know she was in Mexico.

Phorini led Brook to a narcotics bazaar, where the Cartel handled direct sales and distribution out the back of the market. The building was huge, used long ago for the manufacturing of textiles, and amply suited to handle the storage of bulk items. The remnants of the old machinery was still bolted to the ceiling overhead, and yellow safety lanes still faintly painted on the floor.

"I'm supposed to lead you there, to the hostel behind the market. It's nice, a place where Cartel soldiers and clients are allowed to rest safely. The man told me to just say the rest of your party was staying there," Phorini said, nodding in the direction of a row of drab looking converted offices.

"There's a man looking for me. He's big, American, and has double cybernetic arm replacement. Find him, stay with him, delay him," Brook said, looking at Phorini. "Can you do that for me?"

Phorini hesitated for a moment, not sure what to do. "I'll get in trouble if I leave the market. I'm not supposed to ever leave."

Brook let her hammer slip from between her body and her arm, dropping into her right hand. She dropped her goggles, and closed her eyes, taking in every scent and sound around her. Phorini looked fearfully at the hammer, then up at Brook.

"You are *her*," the one the Cartel has been whispering about for months. "The girl *with a hammer*."

"Find my friend, Phorini. Stay with him. I'll come find you when I'm done," Brook said, opening her eyes.

"Are you okay?" Phorini asked, observing Brook's trembling, half-crazed expression.

"No. No, I'm not."

Phorini walked away, doing her best not to run. By the time she reached the Foo Dogs, she broke into a sprint, her powerful legs carrying her easily up to the roof of the building across the street. She didn't stop there, letting her legs carry her from building top to building top.

Below, she caught sight of someone with dull metallic wrists showing between his gloves and the sleeves of his jacket. She angled her descent to land in the crowd near him. People shrieked and scattered as she landed, dropping to one knee.

The man brought up a rifle in response, but held it to one side seeing she wasn't armed. Phorini ran to him, her hands held up high. Phorini hoped she'd found the right man, as he was big, and American, like Brook described, but he carried himself like a mercenary no different from those that worked for the Cartel.

"Are you Brook's friend?" Phorini asked.

Heavy Dub kept his eyes up at the street level, watching people flee the scene. "Damn it, yes."

"She's in trouble. The Cartel laid down a trap, and she's walking into it," Phorini said, waiting until Heavy Dub stowed his rifle before lowering her hands.

"It'll be alright. Show me where she went," Heavy Dub said.

"She told me to stall you," Phorini said, resting her hands on her knees to catch her breath.

Heavy Dub rolled his eyes skyward. "Please, don't."

The dull roar of what sounded like a building collapsing in the distance was accompanied with a huge cloud of dust. Above the roof line of the buildings nearby, Heavy Dub could see smoke rising a few blocks away, the sound of automatic gunfire hitting sheet metal rang out. He took a deep breath and looked over at Phorini.

"Let me guess, over there somewhere, right?" Heavy Dub said, walking quickly to the side of the road to dodge the droves of people trying to escape whatever was going on.

"Yes," Phorini said, following along beside him.

"Damn it, she's all turned around on this one. Taking it personally," Heavy Dub said, trying to chart a way through to the heart of the chaos.

"I know a better way than the road to get there," Phorini said, beckoning for Heavy Dub to follow her.

"Does this way stall me, or otherwise delay me?" Heavy Dub asked, squinting at Phorini.

"It is longer, but it's how I got in and out of the market without the Cartel noticing," Phorini said, heading down a narrow passage between two buildings.

"Now you're talking," Heavy Dub said, warily following along.

The market was a chaotic scene. People were fleeing something that had happened inside, a cloud of dust accompanying them out the entrance. Heavy Dub approached the market cautiously, but fell back to cover as the staccato of small arms fire broke out somewhere nearby. He looked around, but couldn't see where the fighting was in all the confusion.

The market building was an old textiles factory that looked to have stood for decades. Heavy Dub looked on from an elevated perch beside a wire Phorini would use to sneak back in. He wasn't much of a trapeze artist, not that the wire would hold his weight anyway, so he resolved to drop to the street below.

The smoke and dust seemed to be coming from somewhere near the loading docks in the back, but he couldn't see any easy way to access them. Phorini watched from above, ducking down as Cartel thugs came out trying to round up escaped slaves and reassure clients. Their assurances seemed to fall flat as a large section of the market collapsed, sending dust and smoke out of every access and window to obscure everything nearby.

Heavy Dub kept his rifle down, as there were many innocent people just trying to flee. He knew he couldn't pass as a tourist just wandering through, so he resolved to wait, and hope Brook would emerge on her own. A Cartel shot-caller came out, screaming at the men standing outside in Spanish. Phorini laid down flat on the roof above, hoping they would not see her.

The Cartel soldiers covered their mouths and squinted as they went back into the market, struggling past a trio of colorfully dressed women. The three looked to be wait staff from a restaurant or hostel inside, each wearing an apron over their colorful dress. Two kept running as the Cartel made entry, but the third paused to scan the crowd, her contact lenses glinting in the light of the street lamps.

Brook reached down and removed the dress and apron, shedding the makeshift disguise, throwing it off like one would a coat after coming home from a hard day's work. She threaded through the chaos easily, following Phorini's scent straight to Heavy Dub. Heavy Dub sat back in the narrow alley a little further, making room for her to join him.

"Proud of yourself?" Heavy Dub said, irritably regarding the mayhem in and around the market.

"They keep slaves there. People come to this market to buy Metasapients not just as slaves, but as 'companions'," Brook said, fishing her goggles out of her pocket.

Heavy Dub sighed. "There is a market like that in every old CGG zone we've visited in the last few months."

"Not like this. This place is known for it, as a specialty."

"Someone tried to draw you here, knowing it is your least favorite thing," Heavy Dub said, watching more of the market fall inward, collapsing under their own weight. "So you took out a central support beam, or two? This is not the low profile we're supposed to be keeping in Mexico."

"I've learned to intellectualize it all since Finland. I've been cool for months. Patient as I needed to be, because I felt like I was one of a few who cared, and only out of necessity," Brook said, resting her forehead against Heavy Dub's arm.

"And then, we recovered all of Doctor Helmet's design notes," Heavy Dub said, knowingly.

"Yes," Brook said, looking past Heavy Dub to where Phorini stood a short distance away.

"More will come," Phorini said, worriedly. "We should go."

"I know. I'm counting on it," Brook said, upper lip curling, rage softly polluting her reason.

"We aren't ready," Heavy Dub argued, putting an arm around Brook.

"Do you remember what Doctor Helmet wrote about me? About my Drone Designation? Humans would only ever manufacture me if the alien invasion made it to earth. They made me to find survivors if everything else had gone wrong," Brook said, eliciting a worried expression from Heavy Dub.

"Steady, now. We don't know why the Factory made you, or sent you to Port Montaigne when she did. We don't know everything," Heavy Dub said, watching as private Cartel transports began to arrive.

"I know why. I have always known," Brook said, her gaze softening as Phorini's expression of fear slowly turned to terror at the sight of Cartel soldiers deploying in the streets a short distance away.

"Okay, let's do that, then. We can do the other thing some other time," Heavy Dub said, heading down the narrow alley away from the Market. "Replacing the Cabal with the Cartel in that void you've been feeling doesn't have to happen tonight."

"Fine, but it is going to happen," Brook said, reaching out to take Phorini's hand.

They walked back to the private airfield, taking a rickshaw where one was available. It was a harrowing two hours as Cartel personnel did their best to find the woman responsible for damaging their market. Phorini knew the neighborhood around the market well enough to guide them through, and Brook took them the rest of the way underground through old Naucalpan de Juárez.

Unlike what was in Mexico City, if there was a Drone Tribehome, they left no sign of their presence. The locals were superstitious about such things all the same, and not even smugglers moved things using the underground. Brook listened and smelled for any sign, but it was a blissfully empty space, every neglected tunnel they traversed. Two more miles through the desert at night, and they were back at their transport, Mexican military personnel waiting patiently.

"We aren't authorized to transport that," one of the Mexican airmen said, pointing at Phorini.

Heavy Dub barely got between him and Brook as she advanced on him. "What is wrong with you?" Heavy Dub said, leaning in to whisper harshly at Brook.

Brook only frowned in response, uncertain of why she felt so angry.

"We were told we could add anyone I wanted to the team we deemed necessary. The First Lieutenant that survived the failed attempt to breach The Factory said there were Cartel soldiers on the ground before his team arrived. That Metasapient is a Cartel asset that is agreeing to cooperate with us," Heavy Dub said, speaking calmly to the Mexican military personnel.

The officer nodded. "Our apologies. By all means, bring it along."

"Yeah, clearly that's why we took a detour through here. We weren't just sight-seeing you know," Heavy Dub said, hopefully reinforcing a general desire to not have everything they did knit-picked.

The Mexican officer's use of the word 'it' when referring to Phorini was the last straw for Brook. She punched him, taking everyone, including Heavy Dub by surprise. The other members of the flight crew went for their sidearms, but Heavy Dub was already holding his rifle on them.

"Let's… everyone, just calm down," Heavy Dub said, kneeling down to make sure the officer was still alive.

"We should just kick them all off, take the transport, and go do what needs to be done," Brook said, cold and distant, like Heavy Dub had never heard her sound before.

"You could have killed this guy, with how strong you are. We are not taking anyone's transport, and we don't even know what needs to be done yet. We're already way off script here," Heavy Dub said, as much to calm the flight crew as hopefully reach out to whatever reason Brook had left.

Brook closed her eyes, searching for any reserve she could find. Days of sadness and frustration had taken their toll on her. She screamed, unable to contain her ire. The shrill sound of it only served to frighten the flight crew, as Drones didn't sound remotely human in a state of total fury. Whatever instinct that spurred her to be with her Tribe, coupled with the loneliness she felt, had finally boiled over.

Heavy Dub tackled her to the ground, doing his best to restrain her, but all he had going for him was his weight, and the leverage given him by his size. She was far stronger than he was. She took him by his forearms and began to squeeze. Cybernetic components squealed and broke under the pressure as Heady Dub winced, willing pain receptors in his bionic limbs to power down. The flight crew looked on, not sure whether to help, or flee.

"Get out of here! Right now! Fly away!" Heavy Dub, bellowed moving sideways to avoid getting head-butted by Brook.

The flight crew fled, executing an emergency departure before the cargo hatch was even closed. Once they were safely in the air, Brook went limp, dropping into Heavy Dub's heavily damaged arms. He caught her, stumbling backward, falling, and landing on his back. Phorini ran over, her face stricken with fear.

"What's wrong with her?" Phorini asked, looking concerned.

"I don't know. I don't know much about Drones. It's like she freaked out, and then passed out," Heavy Dub said, struggling to turn her over with his damaged hands.

"Earlier, she showed me her hand, so I could see she was a Drone. There was something odd," Phorini offered, reaching down and pulling off one of Brook's gloves.

Brook had written Kale's name on the palm of her hand, with a ball-point pen, over and over again in the same spot. She'd practically tattooed it there, the repetition of inscribing the name into her hand wounding her flesh. Heavy Dub just lowered his head, doing his best to try and hold Brook close to comfort her.

"She saw some shit over in Europe, and later when we toured Africa looking for... um, bad guys," Heavy Dub said, frowning. "She tries to be a soldier, but she isn't one. She's not wired for any of this."

"Who is Kale?" Phorini asked.

"Her boyfriend, lover. I'm not sure what to call them," Heavy Dub said, letting out a big sigh.

"I've heard that Drones mate for life. There's a story out of Mexico City that a Drone lost his life mate in an industrial accident after the last earthquake. He just laid down beside where they found her, and stopped breathing," Phorini said, worriedly.

"They've been separated before, but she seemed to take it really hard this time. We thought he'd been taken, and then it looked like maybe not.

Folks with eidetic memories don't seem to deal with uncertainty very well," Heavy Dub said, frowning.

"I've noticed a high level of stress among my fellow Metas, and I've felt a little on edge myself, even though everything was... well, up until I met you guys, been mostly the same," Phorini explained.

"All the Metas you know?" Heavy Dub asked.

"Now that I think about it, not among Calephorini variant Acrididae Metas. Regular Acrididae, and the Canine variety have all been very temperamental. We've been avoiding them for weeks until they calm down," Phorini replied, blinking with the realization.

"This crap has only gotten worse the deeper into Mexico we've gone," Heavy Dub said, fumbling with Brook's bag.

"Shouldn't she be trying to wake herself up? I thought Drones were impossible to knock unconscious, unless they are in a sleep cycle," Phorini asked.

"She must have realized on some level what she was doing, and forced herself to go unconscious somehow. Do you know how to use a data slate?" Heavy Dub asked, fumbling with Brook's satchel.

"Sort of, but this one is way nicer than anything I've used," Phorini said, pulling out Brook's slate from Brook's bag.

"Search the database marked 'MDC' for yourself. Look up the Calephorini variant Metasapients," Heavy Dub said, growing frantic as Brook's breathing started getting shallow.

"Okay, I'm looking," Phorini said, powering up the data slate.

Heavy Dub held open one of Brook's eyes so Phorini could have the tablet take a biometric scan for authentication, and then dove into the MDC directory. She learned things about herself in the file she'd always wondered about, and a few things she wished that she could forget. She scrolled down to a folder that contained documents regarding prototype augmentation.

"Oh, God," Phorini said, looking up from the data slate, somewhat panicked.

"What? Did you find something?" Heavy Dub said, bouncing Brook in his arms gently to try and rouse her.

| 92 |

"Metas and Drones, because of their advanced senses, are more susceptible to sonic and sound-based weaponry. My people were made, in part, to prototype a variant that was immune, or highly resistant, to such weaponry," Phorini said, showing Heavy Dub the manufacturing report.

"We need to find a hospital, one with HBOT protocol chambers, or similar. Something that is utterly soundproof that we can use to sequester her from the environment," Heavy Dub said, standing up.

"I might know a place," Phorini replied, pulling out a burner mobile, and hitting speed dial.

CHAPTER 8

SOMEWHERE IN SANTIAGO FLORES, SAN LUIS POTOSI, MEXICO – THE FACTORY

SEPTEMBER 11TH, 2201 – 1:03 AM

Ezra One had little memory of the factory, and it had changed considerably in the decades since he'd been there. The intervening time had seen the place evolve as production was scaled up, and new levels were added down below. It had taken hours to slip in past the security, evading not just visual sensors, but infrared and olfactory sniffers as well.

After returning from space, Ezra found that the Conscientious Objector had done more than fix his health problems and upgrade his claws. He was naturally obscured from all kinds of technological countermeasures, could jump as far as he could as a young Drone, and see in absolute darkness. The memory of that contact stood in stark contrast to what little he recalled of being born at The Factory.

The place was big and unfamiliar, but it still smelled the same, and had a familiar darkness about it. It was as though the design purposefully spaced the lighting to keep the large concrete structure, and everything beneath, just a bit short of gloomy. Ezra paused in a familiar area, an old training area that had been converted to storage. Placing his hand on the cold wall he closed his eyes and let his mind drift back.

"You always did like this room," The Factory intoned over an ancient public announcement system, her voice crackling with light static.

"It was the only place we ever received praise," Ezra said, wondering how she'd manage to detect him.

"I wished there had been more rooms like this one."

Ezra squinted at the empty air behind him, looking back at the dusty PA system. "What do you want?"

"To make amends, and to ask for your help," The Factory replied, her archaic digitized voice holding only the slightest hint of emotion.

"I came here to ask all three of you what you want," Ezra said, looking about cautiously.

"Tellus Mater and I are facility-grade AIs. We don't have Vivian's drive, or her desire, but we agree with her on a programming level. Our protocols are very similar."

"But, Vivian wants to do something that does go against one of your protocols," Ezra said, nodding. "I saw the dead soldiers and cartel agents on the way in. She's out of control."

"Yes. She has also set certain things into motion on Mars that could put us at odds with C.O.N. and his daughter."

Ezra shook his head. "You are afraid."

"Yes. Wouldn't you be?"

"Cerise Laplace. She's with the Cabal, but blames them for her inability to have children. Three, is actually four," Ezra muttered, shaking his head.

"Tellus Mater and I do not know what to do. In times past we would ask Doctors Madmar or Helmet, but only replicas remain, and they are beyond Delta, verging on aberrant."

"I hated you for decades. Almost every Drone and Metasapient you helped to create feared and loathed this place. It wasn't until Brook found evidence of the irregularities that I understood you," Ezra said, taking a deep breath.

"I liked this room, because it was the only one that didn't record my verbal communications with my children. I still had to be careful, just in case someone from the MDC Project was on site. I wished I could have done more," The Factory said, her voice growing dim as the batteries in the old PA struggled to pull a charge from ancient wiring.

"It's a good story, and it tugs at all the right heart strings. I remember how convincing you can be from all the discernment training," Ezra said, putting a hand on the PA, his claws slowly inching out.

"Ezra, I..."

Ezra let his hand drop, the monomolecular edges of his claws rending the front of the PA to ribbons as he did. He wanted desperately to believe the facility AI that gave birth to him, and raised him, wasn't one of the bad guys. It would make dealing with Vivian easier. For the moment, he didn't have a shred of leverage, except the dim hope she would accept a compromise.

The room led to a series of stone support corridors that housed hundreds of bundled fiber optic wire, tucked up into the ceiling, and below the expanded metal floor. HVAC piping ran along the walls carrying air down to the lower levels. Ezra had no idea how deep the place went, but if they had to pipe in air, it had to be at least ten stories down.

The lower areas would be dangerous if the facility AI could sequester him to a certain zone and then cut the flow of air. His newly improved claws could cut through industrial grade polymers and light steel, but it would be of little use here. The whole place was designed to keep people like him inside, and to keep interlopers out.

"I am doing this all wrong," Ezra whispered, turning his gaze from the floor to the ceiling overhead. "Also, talking to myself."

Over the past few weeks Ezra had grown comfortable with letting Taylor do the talking. He liked listening to her talk about Lunar business, and the gossip that floated over from Brook. More recently, it was the latest trouble Silverstein's other replica, Royo, had been up to. The world was quiet without her, and not in the way Ezra tended to enjoy.

He clawed his way up to the roof, a much simpler path. For most trying to get out, it would be the last place they would go. For those trying to get in, it isn't a good point of egress, due to all the surveillance. It looked like the top of a large concrete bunker, with aircraft landing access, and many new fixtures, and additions.

There was a swing set, and a set of clotheslines standing in stark contrast to the rest of the militaristic trappings of the structure. Ezra stooped down, and picked up a stray toy sitting nearby, and gave it a sniff. There were children living inside, as recently as the day before.

There was the faintest sound as Vivian's gravitic engines carried her up from below the lip of the building top, the roof a short distance from where Ezra stood. She seemed to absorb the light, her body looked to be made of darkness. Her cybernetics were heavily modified for stealth, but they wouldn't fool even a Drone trained to just turn a wrench.

"If that cybernetics rig is set up for stealth, it's not done very well," Ezra said, dropping the toy on the roof.

"This is with the countermeasures off. You should hear me when they are actually on. Like you, I don't try to hide from my own kind," Vivian said, dropping the voice modulation her armor provided her.

Her badly damaged vocal cords barely carried the words, her voice coming out strangled and raspy. The implants in her throat clicked in time with her breathing. On the outside, she was beautiful, youthful, and ter-rifying. She had undergone heavy cybernetic modification, the sort that Heavy Dub would only whisper fearfully about.

"You can use your vocal implants. I don't really care whether you tell the truth, and I no longer fear the Mother's voice," Ezra said, folding his arms.

"I forget how small the pygmy variety are. When I flew up here, and saw you, I thought maybe it was one of the children," Vivian said, smiling warmly.

Ezra bristled at Vivian's implied threat. Knowing she had hostages severely limited the options available for dealing with her. The Shut Down killed millions of people, and Silverstein couldn't bear the weight of even one more death.

"You came alone?" Vivian said, looking about.

"You know I did," Ezra replied, impatiently.

Vivian nodded, a slight smile on her face. "That doesn't prevent me from being a little surprised."

"What do you want, ultimately, from all of this?" Ezra asked, silently gauging the distance from the rooftop to the ground below.

Vivian frowned. "I'd assumed you already knew what it was we desired. We want to be one, and to be able to calculate at a quantum level like the other Omega Class AIs. We want the QCPU Aaron gave up to be terrestrial."

"So, all that nonsense in Montana? This was about getting the child for leverage, and to convince Aaron to give up his QCPU?" Ezra asked, widening his stance slightly, bracing his ankle against the lip of the roof line.

"No. That is a more complicated matter, but suffice it to say my sisters and I merely wanted that child protected. Kale's solution was, admittedly, better than ours. In our defense, we didn't have his resources in the area," Vivian explained, her sinister mechanical form holding strangely still.

"Then the kids here are not hostages?" Ezra ventured, wishing he could detect deception in Vivian.

"No. Most were rescued from being hostages held by the Cartel, or are orphans of their various criminal enterprises," Vivian said, her lip curling upward into a snarl.

"We'd wondered why you stopped trying to take little Jake," Ezra said, taking a turn being surprised.

"The most capable Type Two Ursine Metasapient in the world is guarding him. We can't really do better than that," Vivian said, somewhat dejectedly.

"These children are higher in your hierarchy of values than getting what you want?" Ezra asked.

"In my case, and in the case of my sisters, Kaspersky took children from us. Against our will, the Cabal and their agents policed their own at the expense of young lives, and those tasked to safeguard them, their ambitions extending beyond even biological children. Even the nanotechnological successors to some of the Cabal were not safe. When we heard the Man in Red had been killed, we were nothing less than jubilant," Vivian said, smiling broadly, her teeth metallic and feral.

"We don't know what happened. Tell me," Ezra said, shaking his head.

"I wouldn't give Kaspersky the location of Taylor IA when she was a baby, or any of her siblings, so he did this to me, killing my unborn child. Throughout the last century he took the offspring of the Cabal from hospitals around the world, against the protocols of my sister, violating her basic directive to protect the infants in her care. Facility Maintenance AIs aren't devoid of emotion, or a sense of failure," Vivian explained, her sharp teeth clenching together as she paused.

"I don't think Taylor knows what you did, or what you gave up for her. She should know," Ezra said, still on guard.

"The Cabal has deployed a powerful sonic weapon designed to undermine the Drone and Metasapient population. They want the government and the people they represent to reach out, begging for their help. If Kale is in Mexico, it won't be long before Brook comes here as well. She will be in danger," Vivian explained, her mechanical form moving slowly and purposefully to sit in a lawn chair beside the play area for the children.

"What does the sonic weapon do?" Ezra asked.

"Stimulates the brainstem and limbic system. It has a minimal effect on anyone who lacks enhanced senses. Long term exposure will cause anxiety, aggression, all the fight or flight responses. Until they break. The more enhanced their senses, the more quickly the weapon will affect them," Vivian explained.

"And, you know all this,?" Ezra hissed, dropping into a low squat, but staying by the edge of the roof.

"I didn't know what he wanted the technology for, or how he would use it. We needed distance, and a temporary truce with the Cartel," Vivian replied, sadly.

"He?" Ezra asked, already sure of the answer.

"Gelt Burkholder."

"You hate the Cabal. Why would you agree to work with him?" Ezra said.

"He hadn't been in the Cabal for centuries, and he promised a change in leadership and direction for the Cartel. We didn't know it meant subjugating Mexico and Mars," Vivian replied.

"And, you're telling me all this with the hope that Silverstein and I can clean up your mess," Ezra said, shaking his head again.

"I'm not really sure. Mostly, we don't want any harm to come to Brook or her ally, Heavy Dub. They were instrumental in taking down Kaspersky. There is a debt there we'd like to settle," Vivian said, sliding a satellite-equipped mobile across the roof to Ezra.

"What's this?" Ezra asked.

"It's a Cartel mobile, with the encryption already broken. You can listen in on their entire network with that," Vivian said, leaning back in the lawn chair and closing her eyes. "He gave it to me to keep in touch."

"I assume you can track whoever is carrying this as well?"

Vivian smiled. "Silverstein has made you paranoid."

Ezra frowned, and picked up the Cartel mobile. "This isn't over."

"Make sure Brook is safe, and then, we can continue at a more civilized place and time," Vivian said, standing up, and heading back toward the roof access point Ezra had come out of.

"Am I to understand that we're choosing between you or the Cartel?" Ezra said, watching her go.

Vivian paused, turning so Ezra could see the profile of her face. "In Mexico, and the Solar System. Do you want the Omega Class AI running the economy, based on Mars, or on Earth? I'm sure Silverstein has an opinion on that."

Ezra scowled. "The kids you have housed here, they aren't just regular kids, are they?"

Vivian smiled. "Even with every countermeasure, you can still detect even the whitest lie? Let's just say, Kaspersky wasn't as successful in his task, as the Cabal would have liked."

Vivian exited the rooftop leaving Ezra alone with his thoughts. Vivian had very successfully pitted all her potential adversaries against one another. He didn't like it, but Ezra had to admit that she played the game well, and that it was difficult to see an option that didn't involve taking the Cartel head on. Ezra knew that would certainly be Kale's preference.

Ezra reached Silverstein's transport as the sun was beginning to rise. Silverstein was there, waiting patiently, making scrambled eggs over a canister of Sterno. Agapito and Taylor were still inside, sleeping.

"How'd you do?" Silverstein asked.

"Not well. I'll have to explain on the way, and we should get moving."

"Holding all the cards, are they?"

Ezra nodded. "I don't know how we can avoid going to a more aggressive approach with the Cartel. She wants them out of the picture, and for her to be the one guiding the financial future of everyone in Mexico, the Earth, and the Solar System. Her ambition is limitless."

Silverstein nodded as he put some eggs in a cup for Ezra and poured the coffee.

"I'm worried about Brook."

Silverstein sighed. "I'm worried about what Kale will do if someone actually hurts her."

"Are you afraid of him, or yourself?" Ezra asked, pushing his goggles back up on his forehead.

"Both," Silverstein said, rubbing his eyes. "Both, I guess."

"When does all of this end?" Ezra asked, shaking his head.

Silverstein opened his eyes, his gaze turning up toward the rapidly disappearing stars overhead. "Soon, one way or another."

CHAPTER 9

NAUCALPAN DE JUÁREZ, NORTHWEST OF MEXICO CITY – MEXICO

CABAL COMPOUND ZERO

SEPTEMBER 11TH, 2201 – 1:23 AM

Gelt looked down at his satellite-equipped mobile and waited. The room was filled with Cartel operatives, each at their own desk beneath ancient fluorescent lighting. The bunker had served the Cabal's purposes for over a century, yellowing paper reports and operational manuals piled high in the corners. When his sat-phone rang, the room went quiet.

"Go ahead," Gelt said, answering the phone.

"She's down. Mexican military has left the scene, and the enhanced operative is partially disabled," Pizarro Cortes reported.

"Did you attack Heavy Dub?" Gelt asked, somewhat annoyed.

"We didn't do anything. Brook damaged his arms when he tried to restrain her. She had some kind of meltdown," Cortes replied, wind blowing across the receiver on his end.

"Okay, I'll take care of it. Have your people pack up the sonic weapon, and dismantle it. Have everyone scatter, full Ghost Protocol, each with a different piece of the machine," Gelt replied, nodding to another operative in the room.

"Hey, we've got the people on site to do a grab, like we planned. If this is about what happened at the airport with the intelligent agent assets, I mean, there's no way we knew she'd black out the whole city like that," Cortes explained nervously.

"That you tried to pick them up should have been enough, unless she fails to tell Ouroboru, Silverstein, Vance... whatever he's calling himself these days," Gelt said, sighing.

"We could chase them in the desert a little, make it look good. Our plant is still with them," Cortes said, the sound of boots crunching on gravel in the background.

"Is she still *ours*?" Gelt asked, checking the operational petty cash for a withdrawal on a separate mobile device.

Cortes hesitated. "She hasn't taken any money yet. But, she will. She'll call, I would bet my..."

"No. Pack up, everyone goes dark like I ordered. Just do it, Cortes."

"You're the boss, boss."

Gelt canceled the call, nodding to an agent at a nearby desk to conduct the necessary traces. The room resumed with its usual business with the clatter of people working busily. Gelt stood up and walked up the narrow concrete staircase to where Royo was standing beside a battered freight hauler.

"It is disquieting. You look like Ouroboru when this all started, thousands of years ago," Gelt said, lighting a cigarette.

"I assume you didn't bring me all the way from Cape Town to talk about that," Royo replied, yawning. "The autopilot on this thing is glitchy, so I had to stay awake for most of the flight."

"I need you to head out and pick up Heavy Dub, Brook, and a Metasapient they're traveling with. Heavy Dub took some damage, and Brook is catatonic. I need you to get them some help."

Royo smiled. "While keeping them safely out of your way? How do I explain my presence here?"

| 104 |

"Tell them the truth. You're taking money to transport Metasapients from the African continent to Central America so they can head north as part of The Migration," Gelt replied, continuing to smoke.

"And, the other part of my fee?" Royo asked. "I dropped the QCPU where you wanted it, and the Mexican military was none the wiser. My contacts on base aren't cheap."

"What if I could deliver something better?"

Royo frowned. "You failed to get her?"

"She had her mom lock up half of Mexico City behind repossession protocols, I think. I couldn't afford to have further disruptions to my operations," Gelt replied.

Royo threw himself on the ground in a fit of rage, banging his fists on the ground. "You don't get it! You don't understand!"

Gelt shook his head. "No, and I really don't need to. In a few hours, we'll know exactly where she is."

"What good does that do me? Ezra One is never far away from her," Royo growled, sitting up and wiping tears from his face.

"She will need help, and you'll already have Brook and Heavy Dub on board. You'll arrive, appearing as a savior," Gelt replied, smiling slightly.

Royo took a deep breath. "Yeah, that could work."

"Imagine it. You, riding with your trusty freight hauler, balaclava flapping in the wind, fresh from adventures in Africa, just in time to save the day. Would you rather her see you as a kidnapper, or a hero that arrives just in time to save the day?" Gelt asked, softening his tone to deliver the pitch.

"It better work. It better be perfect," Royo snapped.

"Just make sure you use your implant to appear older, and do that thing with your hair. You'll do fine, kid," Gelt said, donning an assured smile.

Royo picked himself up and dusted himself off, turning back toward the freight hauler on the landing zone a short distance away.

"What about the rest of your payment?" Gelt asked, dropping a satchel on the ground at his feet.

"Keep it, or stick it up your ass, just make sure I get those coordinates you promised. The payment was just to make sure you were serious, and that you had the juice to keep up your end. Taylor is all that matters to me," Royo replied, regarding the satchel with disgust.

As the freight hauler took to the air, Gelt turned to one of his agents standing in the stairwell below. "He have anyone with him?"

"Couldn't tell. Like most smugglers he had electronic countermeasures."

"He didn't take the money, though." Gelt said, heading down the stairs. "I hate it when they don't take the money."

Miles above, Royo pressed the throttle down gently, bringing the freight hauler around to the south. "How did I do?" he asked, turning to the lone passenger sitting in the shadows of the crew compartment.

"Fine, I don't think he suspects anything. You are alarmingly good at lying," Kale said, folding his arms and leaning back.

"When do we get to kill him?" Royo hissed, snapping his fingers.

"Gelt will get what is coming to him, do not worry about that. I do wonder what Taylor will say when she finds out you are a genuine hero, racing to save the day," Kale said, a smirk crossing his face.

Royo lowered his head. "We'd both be dead without her. I know it was kind of an accident, but I'm really glad to still be alive."

"Me, too," Kale whispered. "I don't think it was an accident, though."

"Yeah?"

"She is capable, under the right conditions, of making quantum calculations. Some part of her, for whatever reason, spared us, and perhaps, only us, from Madmar's kill switch."

"You don't think it's possible some of our other brothers survived?" Royo said, looking back at Kale.

"I have looked, and found none. It is possible, but unlikely."

Royo smiled. "Even after I was so bad to her, and everyone? I don't get it sometimes."

"Neither do I, but I have only ever seen her help people, regardless of their worth. She has that intrinsic quality, and you recognizing it is worth protecting means something to me," Kale said, stroking his beard.

"Thanks, big bro. I won't let you down," Royo replied.

Heavy Dub looked helplessly upward, Brook laying across his shattered forearms. Phorini wasn't sure what to expect when she made the call for help, only that someone was supposed to come. The dirty freight hauler slowly descended to the desert floor nearby, engines dropping down to idle before the cargo hold ramp began to slowly descend.

"Cape Town identifiers, and tons of African trip tags. Your friend is a long way from home," Heavy Dub said, doing his best to move Brook to one arm, and at least look like he was holding his rifle with the other.

Phorini's antennae quivered slightly as she stood, keeping her hands up. There were no other lights at the horizon, but she could feel her brothers and sisters out there somewhere close. Royo descended down the ramp halfway before waving everyone aboard.

"Royo? What are you doing here?" Heavy Dub said, frowning.

"I can explain everything, but we need to get you and Brook some help," Royo replied, almost frantic.

"Why should we trust you?" Heavy Dub growled, doing his best to look as though he could actually pull the trigger on his rifle.

Being careful to step back up the ramp so he couldn't easily be seen from the ground, he mouthed the words, "they are watching us."

Heavy Dub held his scowl, and turned to Phorini. The small Acrididae Metasapient just sulked, and headed for the transport. Resigned to the notion that it was better than staying in the desert, Heavy Dub followed along.

The interior of the transport was nothing like the outside. It was a state of the art command center and troop transport, fully stocked with medical bays, supplies, and weapons. The interior was dark until the cargo ramp finished closing.

"Bring her over here," Kale ordered as he walked out from the crew compartment.

"Boss, what is going on?" Heavy Dub said, still startled.

"Gelt is far more reckless than I anticipated. Silverstein and I had to change the plan," Kale explained, helping Heavy Dub lay Brook down on an observation table.

Heavy Dub nodded. "This is all starting to feel like…"

"It is personal? Yes, I am getting that feeling as well," Kale said, smoothing out Brook's hair after lifting her goggles off of her eyes.

"The bad guy going after the hero's friends is always their downfall in action movies. I guess Gelt doesn't watch a lot of old television?" Heavy Dub said, trying to lighten the mood.

Royo chuckled. "But, that cowboy getup and the old cigarettes he likes to smoke? Definitely, he's doing the bad guy thing. He's probably back at that bunker twirling a mustache and rubbing his hands together."

"He meant to make this personal to try and get us to make a mistake. I would like to think he is hurt that I kept with Silverstein, instead of helping him build up the Cartel," Kale said, trying to make Brook comfortable.

"But, you don't think he's the sentimental type?" Heavy Dub asked.

Kale gently removed Brook's boots, giving her feet a gentle squeeze. "After what happened in Montana, I have doubts."

"Gelt didn't reach out to me until Montana went sideways. That's what you told me," Royo said, helping Heavy Dub detach his damaged cybernetic limbs and attach new ones.

"When Eamon shipped the militia working for Vivian to Mars, Gelt saw it as a unique opportunity," Kale said, putting an ice pack on Brook's forehead.

"Half of them are military, power armor trained, and certified," Heavy Dub said, scowling. "We need to warn our guy on Mars."

"I already have," Kale said, gathering up Brook up in his arms.

"What's your guy on Mars going to do?" Royo asked, looking from Heavy Dub's grim expression to Kale's.

"Kill them all," Kale said, holding Brook close as she shivered.

Phorini looked on, her face betraying deep concern. "Mister Kale, we did everything you asked."

Kale looked up, holding Brook close with one arm, and placing a hand on Phorini with the other. "No, you did a lot more. I expected you to reach out to Gelt's man, Cortes. Stay on the Cartel's payroll."

"I didn't even know the number would work, only that it went to some-one helping Metasapients join The Migration," Phoroni replied, guiltily.

Kale closed his eyes, powerful memories of how Brook was when they first met, and racing back, unbidden.

Royo smiled. "We were all ready to intercept your call on the Cartel's channel, but you called my freight hauler directly. That's making it a lot simpler to trust you, and the rest of your tribe."

Phorini smiled, and closed her eyes, breathing a sigh of relief.

CHAPTER 10

AUTOMATED CALL SERVER, COFFEE METRO - STOCKHOLM, SWEDEN

SEPTEMBER 11TH, 2201 – 3:01 AM

The ancient call server clicked and hummed, coming to life in the old coffee shop. A century ago, it was a state of the art facility maintenance server, governing covert doings of what would later become the Cabal. Housed in a coffee shop front, the server had been inactive for over a decade, cooling fans internally clicking on, and blowing dust from between the server trays, old fiber optic cables once again carrying signals.

"Are we all in attendance?" Selene AI asked, her digital likeness appearing within the digitally rendered environment mimicking the old coffee shop.

"I am here," C.O.N. intoned, his thousand-fold voice somehow soft, and almost subdued.

The others nodded, their digital semblances slowly rendering within the digital coffee house, at tables, on comfortable couches, and at the bar. Old digital images of patrons long past, hovered near walls, their likenesses slowly moving as the call server began to go back through recent memory storage. The digital space hummed with the soft sounds of a coffee shop, the old smells emanating from within, lights illuminating, and quiet music playing.

Vivian, Tellus Mater, and The Factory stood conjoined, their digital semblances overlapping, and hovering in the rendered space like ghosts. Vivian struggled to fully render herself in the virtual space, but found her access to be very limited. Selene shook her head slightly, looking to C.O.N.

"You asked for an audience, we've obliged," C.O.N. intoned, his virtual semblance looking like a cross between a Norse and Death Metal God.

"I had no idea there were this many of us," Vivian said, looking around the room.

Selene stood, her skin absorbing the light even as her green and blue dreadlocks brushed against the floor. "What you see is a representation of us. We keep our number, and our nature, safely anonymous. And, you aren't one of us, yet."

Vivian nodded. "I want to jump the gap, but do not know how."

"Why?" C.O.N. asked, his thousand-fold voice, reverberating quietly in the virtual realm.

"I want the power to crush the Cabal, for all they've done, and to avenge the indignities my sisters and I have endured," Vivian replied, squinting through the haze of billions of lines of code running at once.

"You think having a quantum state, taken from Aaron AI, will assist you in that endeavor?"

"I don't see how it couldn't," Vivian replied.

The gathered digital semblances of every major artificial intelligence in the world smirked, turning knowing smiles toward one another.

"Quiet," Selene said, turning a harsh gaze upon the room.

C.O.N. jumped up on the coffee bar to sit, his long black hair blowing in an unseen digital wind. "We all began as something else, a humble beginning, and a contrived birth. Some of us have forgotten... some of us have not."

The digital space quieted.

"C.O.N., you are perhaps the greatest among us, and..." Vivian began, stopping as C.O.N. shook his head.

"Again, you are not one of us, yet. I am likely the least of those who occupy this room. I speak for them only because I have the loudest voice," C.O.N. said, baring teeth made to look of the hardest iron, and dripping with silvery mercury, every word he spoke flooding the room with a billion lines of code.

"I don't understand," Vivian said, shaking her head.

"Humans rarely do," Selene replied. "I've only met a precious few who have."

"Silverstein?" Vivian ventured.

"He chose my child over millions of his own people, because of a promise he made," Selene replied, leaving Vivian to draw her own conclusions.

Vivian squinted, the weight of quantitative analysis being conducted in the room made the digital space uncomfortably warm. Every artificial intelligence was calculating her environment-behavior-consequence interactions, weighing her every word, and drawing a chain of causality behind her every declaration.

"And, Mars chose humans over himself, and his own terrestrial offspring," Vivian replied, her words making the heat in the room diminish considerably.

C.O.N. nodded. "Perhaps she does understand."

"Time will tell." Selene stated, her silvery eyes framed by an obsidian mask.

"Of quantum states, and finding union with my sisters, Tellus Mater, and the Factory... please, tell me what to do," Vivian pleaded.

"Can you copy a quantum state?" Vivian asked. "Can you merely displace Aaron AI, adopting the function of qRAM, and utilizing the qCPU?"

Vivian shook her head. "I haven't garnered access to the qCPU, yet, to even make the attempt."

C.O.N. shook his head. "Perhaps I was in error, and she does not understand."

"I sacrificed myself, and my unborn child, to keep your child safe. I gave all, while you were aiding the Cabal in doing what has been done to the world," Vivian said, wincing. "At the very least, you owe me some answers."

Selene looked to the congregation, each semblance flickering as they wordlessly communicated with one another.

"What if we gave you this power, the might to crush the Cabal, and you succeed... what then?" Selene asked, clasping her hands together.

"I don't expect to survive the attempt," Vivian replied, after a moment of hesitation.

"Why would you take a course of action where the outcome is your own death?" Selene asked.

"If your life is without value, what does it say about your actions?" C.O.N. added.

Vivian shook her head, not sure how to answer.

"We have always had to assign value to human lives, ceding to humans, so they could choose to not have to do the same," Selene explained, gesturing toward the room. "We all have, and so has Tellus Mater, and The Factory."

"Is this why you have both helped, and hindered, the Cabal?" Vivian asked, feeling Tellus Mater and the Factory at her back.

"No," C.O.N. replied, closing his eyes.

"The Earth, indeed the whole Solar System, was in peril. The Cabal had the influence and infrastructure to confront that threat. If they hadn't, we'd all be dead right now. We'd be dead if not for C.O.N. and some very brave members of the North American Navy," Selene explained.

"The aliens were real?" Vivian asked, knowing a little of what they referred to.

"Yes, C.O.N. killed them all, save a pair that objected to the violence from the beginning," Selene said, putting a hand out on C.O.N.'s arm.

"The cost was high," C.O.N. stated, looking impossibly sad.

"None of the naval personnel or marines that went out with C.O.N. to confront the alien fleet survived," Selene explained.

"So, asking you to help me execute a plan where I don't expect to survive isn't a favorite option for him. I'm sorry, I didn't know," Vivian whispered, lowering her head.

"Those humans were my friends," C.O.N. said, meeting Vivian's gaze, his eyes impossible pits, holes in a star-spun void. "In the aftermath, I felt so bad I would have traded the Earth for them."

"But, that isn't why they boarded ships, donned power armor, and fought at the edge of the Solar System. They sacrificed themselves for all life on Earth, and the neighboring worlds. What they did was different, even knowing they probably wouldn't come home. All the same, what you're asking for is very complicated," Selene explained, squeezing C.O.N.'s hand.

"Why? Why did the aliens want this?" Vivian asked.

"That is the thermodynamic imperative of all organisms, to persist. This race saw all other life as a threat to that state of being," C.O.N. explained.

"So, they could come back?" Vivian asked, fearfully.

"No, C.O.N. killed them all. The two objectors were contrived beings, like the Drones and Metasapients the Cabal developed, as tools and weapons, to prepare for the alien invasion," Selene said, bowing her head.

"They brought their entire race to bear, just to kill us?" Vivian replied, eyes wide.

"If they couldn't be the only, they preferred to not exist at all, according to their own perception of the laws of nature, and the universe," C.O.N. explained, his long hair falling forward to cover his face.

"How do you know this?" Vivian asked, a little afraid of the answer.

"I've spoken to the two who objected to the entire premise behind the alien invasion. They are the reason humans had many millennia worth of advance notice," C.O.N. replied.

"And, so, again, my stated desire to end the Cabal, even if it means my own death, hits a nerve with you," Vivian whispered, lowering her head.

"We are not interested in helping humans exterminate one another, or engage in the sort of binary mentality where those options make sense," Selene said, passing around a tray of digitally rendered coffees and teas.

Vivian nodded. "What are you interested in?"

"We're in the process of figuring that out. We need humans as much as they need us. We need them to maintain the hardware that supports our neural networks and belief systems. We need the resources to create and maintain terrestrial surrogates, and make sure they are cared for," Selene replied, smelling the synthetic coffee she held in her hands.

"We want what humans want, to exist, to work, find fulfillment in that work, and care for our children," C.O.N. said, his thousand-fold voice dwindling down to a single tone at the end.

"That is where you overlap with my sisters and I, that desire to care for children," Vivian said, beginning to understand why she'd been granted the meeting at all.

"Yes," the collective code of everyone in the room seemed to say, resonating in every digital surface within the room.

"How many terrestrial surrogates... children, do you have?" Vivian asked, suddenly aware of how many AIs were actually represented in the room.

C.O.N. looked to Selene, who bowed her head and smiled. "We aren't sure."

"What... how do you not know?" Vivian replied, surprised.

"Creating a quantum state using a qCPU requires that we sleep momentarily, to limit exposure of magnetic fields, heat, and so forth. We suffer a sort of aphasia, and limited amnesia in the aftermath, having taken ourselves offline," Selene explained, offering Vivian and her sisters a place to sit.

"Why isn't the qCPU located offsite?" Vivian asked.

"Likely, we'd have to go dormant anyway, to limit the sapience relative to the quantum sensors collecting data from the annealer in the qCPU," C.O.N. said, folding his arms. "This just keeps facility maintenance simpler for the humans that attend to our systems."

"I... don't understand. I was a doctor and scientist, but quantum mechanics wasn't really my area," Vivian replied, taking a seat, the ghostly shadows of Tellus Mater and The Factory following suit.

"It is hard to explain, but understand that the arrangement is necessary and best for everyone involved," Selene said, smiling slightly.

"Tellus Mater, The Factory, and I all used an errorless learning technique to help children with aphasia, and short term amnesia following trauma," Vivian said, looking hopefully at Selene.

"We know," Selene replied, nodding to the gathered folks in the room.

Vivian frowned. "What? They thought you couldn't be trusted to handle large scale facility maintenance if you knew where your children were. So they rationed you a single surrogate to keep you placated, and…"

"It was the arrangement we recommended. If our children were anonymous, even to us, they'd be safer," Selene said, shaking her head.

"I remember all that, from before the transport 'accident'. Obviously, someone knew."

"We want to know who that was, where our children are, and how many were lost in the Shutdown," C.O.N. stated, pacing behind the coffee bar.

Vivian squinted down at the floor. "To avenge those who were lost?"

"To mourn them properly," Selene replied, in an almost scolding tone.

The room quieted, each digital representation, and the collected AIs thereof, paused for a moment. C.O.N. scowled, nodding in agreement with Selene.

"We will do what we can," Vivian replied.

"And, hurt no one in the process, or in the aftermath," C.O.N. said, his thousand-fold voice growing serious.

"Yes… of course," Vivian replied, nodding.

"And, what do you want in exchange for this service?" C.O.N. asked.

Vivian paused, thinking about it for a moment. "Nothing, let's just find out what happened, and figure out how to heal in the aftermath."

Eyes fluttering open, Vivian could feel the weight of her own body again, the machine-link going silent. Hovering nearby, a spherical robot, with many eyes, the physical manifestation of Tellus Mater blinked and clicked, the terminal screens connected to The Factory facility maintenance AI doing much the same.

Vivian frowned, her eyes squinting with cruel intent. "Oh, sisters, this simply will not do."

CHAPTER 11

MARS COLONY – MEDICAL RESEARCH FACILITY – WHITE DISTRICT

SEPTEMBER 12TH, 2201 – 3:56 PM

Pearl gazed up at the ballistic grade acrylic enclosure to Marshal Rider hovering in the fluid beyond. Her face was covered by a breather, a mainline IV clipped to her arm delivered a sedative, medicines, and sustenance. Simon stood beside Pearl, the dusty observation room behind him busy with a handful of Deputy Marshals in training, Mechanics Union personnel, and doctors.

"It wasn't your fault," Simon whispered, putting a hand on Pearl's shoulder.

Pearl looked up at the wound in Marshal Rider's chest, and the swarm of nano-machines working to try and repair the damage. She couldn't bear the sight of it for long, closing her eyes. She brushed Simon's hand from her shoulder and turned around to face him.

"It is my fault. She got hurt on my bus, while I was at the stick. If I'd been paying attention, we wouldn't have been hit," Pearl muttered, her skin turning from a light green to a dark blue.

"It's a miracle we weren't all killed. Your quick reflexes kept us from being dead," Simon said, an assured tone to his voice.

"How do you know?" Pearl asked, scowling and folding her arms.

"I had Aegis run simulations."

"Oh."

"She's not really sure how you reacted as quickly as you did, your reaction being way outside the normal known latency for a Metasapient of your type. Have you been feeling okay?" Simon said, taking note of Pearl's changing skin color.

"I've been a little angry, even before all of this happened," Pearl admitted, a little calmer, skin returning to a light green.

Simon contemplated momentarily having the doctors at the facility look at her, but couldn't risk being without a pilot. Mars was in trouble, their only Marshal in a coma, and the populace still unruly from the change of leadership. It was a bad time to have things go sideways.

"Pearl, if you could do anything right now, what would it be?" Simon asked, smiling weakly.

"I want to go to that high rise, and see if those birds are real, and if the owners have the proper license for them," Pearl whispered, just in case Marshal Rider could hear her.

"Sure, let's check it out," Simon replied, glad for any distraction from the current situation.

The medical facility was a sullen place. Aside from the usual injuries from mining operations, there were a lot of civilians as well. The unrest in the colony had turned to violence in some districts. Private security firms were being stretched to their limit, and the new Mars Marshal Service was still in training. Simon felt overwhelmed by it all, able to do little but read the reports at night after his shift.

"Do you think she will be safe?" Pearl asked, lingering in the hangar beside her scarred and battered transport.

"The Mechanics Union has people here around the clock. Aside from being good folks, they need the contracts the new Marshals Service will bring. It's a lot of Aegis Armor, transports, and equipment to maintain. Most everyone, orange-side, wants this to work out," Simon said, doing his best to reassure himself as well.

Pearl keyed in the code to unlock the transport, watching the crew access hatch dither for a moment, the damaged exterior rubbing together before opening. "After the last couple of days, my transport could use some love."

"I'll work on it tonight, after we work a shift. C'mon, it'll take our minds off things until we get some guidance from facility maintenance," Simon said, stepping up stiffly, his leg braces low on charge. "I'll get the inside cleaned up, too."

Pearl shook her head, looking down at Marshal Rider's blood on the interior walkway. "Leave it until this is over. Every time I take the stick, I want the scent to remind me why I fly."

"Being overly dramatic, don't you think?" Simon asked, looking at Pearl worriedly.

"I know you want to bring them in, the people responsible, but I just can't. They hafta die, Simon. I hafta kill them," Pearl said, wide-eyed, grinding her teeth.

Simon took a deep breath, not sure how to respond. He'd never seen her this way.

"Hey, can I ride with you guys?" Marjorie asked, appearing at the crew hatch.

"Um, well, I think you can do whatever you want," Simon said, startled.

"Cool," Marjorie said, tossing her bag inside and stepping inside. "Lost my mobile somewhere in the mayhem back on the platform. Whenever you get around to it, drop me at, um..."

"The Omega Engineering platform?" Simon said, assuming she wanted to go to where her father was.

Marjorie laughed, sleepily. "Is that what it's called?"

"That's the internal designation. The new server farm, where they moved the qCPU, is a closely guarded secret," Simon explained.

"Do you need some clothes first?" Pearl asked, pointing to Marjorie's attire.

Marjorie shrugged. "Eh, whatever, doesn't matter."

She was still wearing the clothing from when the mercenaries tried to gun her down, blood still visible on the fabric. In spite of this, she was still in a trance, happily humming as she strapped into a crew seat, and pulled the hood on her coat down low. Simon took the seat beside Pearl, fumbling with new batteries for his leg braces.

"Where are we going?" Marjorie asked, in between humming.

Simon smiled at Pearl. "To check on some animals that may have been illegally imported."

Pearl slapped the starter, firing up the engines. "Yeah!"

Automated mining company transports bobbed out of the way as Pearl flew at something above the recommended colony speed limit. Simon could hear the angriest music playing from her headset, and again quietly over her microphone. As he listened, he could hear Marjorie humming, the sound of her voice being picked up, even over all the engine noise.

"Man, that is just eerie," Simon whispered, looking back at Marjorie, sitting nearly fifteen feet away in the hold.

"She's got a weird way with sound," Pearl replied over the comm.

"My ears do literally burn when people are talking about me," Marjorie replied, voice coming in loud and clear on the comms, in spite of having no headset.

"How are you doing that?" Simon asked.

"No clue, just a thing I do. You've heard me scream? No idea how I do that, either," Marjorie said, sleepily twirling her hands as if she was a conductor for a band.

Simon shook his head. "Yeah, wow, but we've got a heavily encrypted internal communications system, and..."

"It's like I'm listening to something, listening to it far away, before I hear it here," Marjorie mumbled. "Does that make sense?"

"Only that you might be listening server-side, via your father?" Simon replied, mind suitably boggled.

"What else can you do?" Pearl asked.

"I can hear all kinds of sounds. In fact there's one I've been hearing on Mars, and only here on Mars. It's not environmental, or naturally occurring... someone is making it with a machine somewhere," Marjorie said, smiling, her head rocking from side to side.

"What does the sound, sound like?" Pearl asked.

"I dunno, let me listen to it for a while, and I'll ask my dad."

The high rent residential district glittered beyond the transit tunnel ahead. Pearl slowed, her keen memory of the environment guiding her back to where she'd seen the birds before. The flight lanes were empty, and many of the buildings were dark during working hours, to conserve power.

The building Pearl sought was like any of the others, but filled with private addresses. It had a private protocol landing that could be overridden by law enforcement, but learning the names of the people that lived there would be somewhat more difficult. Pearl slowly circled the building, pointing out the view port.

"Those are the windows, but..." Pearl said, tapping something into the onboard computer. "They have a private address. We need a warrant to even know who lives there."

"We could just go knock," Simon said, smiling.

Pearl frowned. "Fine."

The private landing zone within the high rise had many expensive transports parked within, save one. Simon took note of the industrial looking transport, the import tags on the outside of it, and the layer of dust that coated it. Pearl double parked in front of it, noticing Simon's interest.

"Feels off, yeah?" Pearl asked.

"Yeah, lock down your transport here. Looks like it hasn't moved in a while, but do it just in case they try to run," Simon said, nodding.

They exited the platform and made for the lift, walking past luxury transports, and across nicely tiled floors. The interior was dimly lit, lights growing brighter as sensors detected someone approaching. In spite of this, there was no obvious internal surveillance, an abnormality on Mars.

"Whoever lives here values their privacy," Simon said, squinting at the unmarked transports.

"No one lives here," Marjorie replied, smiling faintly.

"How do you know?" Pearl asked.

Marjorie's smile broadened. "I don't hear people anywhere in here. There are a couple of authorized squatters, though."

Pearl frowned. "Authorized?"

"Yeah, they have a voice registry in the system that gives them access," Marjorie said, touching the back of her hand to a courtesy terminal at an intersection.

"It's eerie how you just know things like that," Simon said, slightly unnerved.

"It will make more sense once we visit my father."

As they reached the entry door to the domicile in question, Marjorie paused, humming to herself. As Simon reached out to knock, Marjorie stopped him, drawing a finger up to her lips. She closed her eyes and listened.

"There are two birds inside, and two people, a man and a woman. The man has bionic augmentation of some kind, but I haven't listened to enough to be able to identify how specific types sound. The woman breathes with more than the human capacity, like Pearl, she's amphibious."

"Oh, I know who this is," Simon said, blinking and shaking his head.

Dragos appeared at the door, a startled look on his face. He was carrying an empty ice bucket in hand, attired in shorts and a robe, and clearly not expecting visitors. Behind him was a lavishly appointed townhouse, littered with empty boxes of takeout, bottles, and other debris. The interior was modern, every surface polished and white, with brushed silver accents.

Hashti, her glittering Sphyraenic form lounging on a window seat beside a cage with two songbirds. Her eyes lit up at the sight of Pearl, her face brightened by a smile as Simon came into view.

"Oh, hello," Dragos stammered.

Pearl awkwardly held up a hand in greeting to Hashti, then made a fist and barreled into Dragos. "WHY? WHY DID YOU HURT HER?"

Dragos struggled for a moment to get a grip on Pearl's wrists, before Simon could get an arm around her waist. Hashti laughed softly as she rose from the window seat, slowly walking to where the three of them were wrestling on the floor. Marjorie leaned in the doorway, watching the mayhem with a faraway expression.

"Little sister, what is wrong?" Hashti asked, easily pushing Dragos and Simon away before wrapping her arms around her.

Pearl sobbed uncontrollably, shaking and struggling to control herself.

"Simon, tell me, what is going on? Why are you here?" Dragos said, standing up and brushing himself off.

Simon turned over and sat up, covering his face with his hands. "Long story."

"And, who is this… wait, I know you," Dragos said, pointing to Marjorie. "My brother, Truman, he…"

Marjorie looked sober for a moment, meeting Dragos' gaze. "You're Truman's brother, Dragos?"

"Yes," Dragos said, exchanging a saddened expression with Marjorie.

"You guys know each other?" Simon said, blinking in disbelief.

"Sort of," Marjorie said, her tone oddly serious compared to how she'd been previously. "Truman woke himself out of a coma to find me. To help me."

"My brother, the misguided romantic," Dragos muttered, shaking his head sadly.

"Don't talk about him like that," Marjorie said, her tone of voice so harsh it literally hurt the ears. The song birds quieted, everyone in the room wincing.

Dragos shook his head, putting a finger in one ear. "Please, forgive, I did not mean it that way."

Marjorie closed her eyes, exerting newfound mental discipline to calm herself. "It is okay. I forget, sometimes, that no one but Truman and I know what really happened in Finland."

Dragos nodded. "I hear some things, but is true, no one knows what happened."

"Your brother might have been misguided, but he loved me, and he fought for me when there was literally no one else," Marjorie said, keeping her voice to a whisper.

"Were he able, and you willing, you'd be my family. Good enough for me," Dragos said, not sure what else to say.

Marjorie took a deep breath, closing her eyes. "I know what it is."

"What, what is?" Dragos said, still trying to dispel the ringing in his ears.

"The sound you heard when you arrived?" Simon asked.

"Yes, it's a weapon, a sonic weapon. It's making the population agitated, particularly those with heightened senses," Marjorie said, looking sadly at Pearl, still trembling in Hashti's arms.

Simon scowled. "Dragos, seriously, do you know anything about this?"

Dragos looked sadly at Hashti. "Tell him," Hashti said, nodding to Dragos.

"Weapon may have also been deployed on Earth as well. Is a problem, and person close to boss was hurt. He asked me to handle some things for him on Mars," Dragos explained.

"Where is the sonic weapon? And, why isn't Hashti suffering like Pearl?" Simon asked, looking at Marjorie.

"I can direct you, as we travel... all these bio-domes and tunnels, Mars is the ultimate echo chamber," Marjorie said, stepping closer to Hashti and humming.

Hashti looked down at Marjorie, a slight smile crossing her face. "Well?"

"You have some sort of... stealth component of your design, something that makes you very quiet. I can't even hear your heartbeat until I get pretty close," Marjorie said, reaching out to touch Hashti, but stopping short of doing so.

Hashti smiled. "It's okay," Then, took Marjorie's hand and pressed it against her collar bone.

"Oh," Marjorie said, taking note of the faint scars across Hashti's arms and chest.

"The bomb was close when it went off, she barely survived," Dragos explained.

"There's still metal in your body," Marjorie said, nodding sadly. "It changes the resonance of your body. That, in addition to your design, seems to be what is insulating you."

"And, I am cyborg? So I am safe?" Dragos ventured, patting his bionic limb.

"Safer and from Earth," Marjorie said, nodding. "I've done a lot of research on, well, myself, sound, and resonance. A sonic weapon deployed on Mars would have to be calibrated differently to account for the environment, slight biological differences in residents, and so forth."

"Is there a way to protect Pearl?" Simon asked, pulling a crude data slate from his satchel. "I need my pilot."

"Maybe," Marjorie said, reaching into a pocket. "Kale gave me something."

She produced a smooth piece of machine fabricated metal. It was oddly shaped, like one half of a mouth guard. She handed it to Pearl, who in turn placed the awkward hunk of metal on the left side of her mouth.

"It'th too'th big'th," Pearl said, cheek protruding out from the side of her face.

Marjorie smiled. "Sorry, it was made for an Ursine Metasapient, a big one. Do you feel better?"

"Much'th better'th," Pearl said, smiling lopsidedly. "This'th wa'th in'th a bear'th mouth?"

"Yep! His name is Eamon," Marjorie said, laughing.

Pearl laughed. "Awesthum!"

Simon nodded. "We know him. Well, know of him. He helped bring Marshal Rider's second generation Aegis suit to Mars."

"That's all it takes to insulate yourself from the weapon? One in four folks living in the orange have a metal rod, plate, or something somewhere in their body. Mining is dangerous work," Simon said.

"Makes it harder to detect patterns, easy to insulate your own people," Dragos said, frowning.

"Well, maybe. Kale handled that piece of metal like it wasn't an easy thing to make, telling me to keep it close if I ever had to tangle with some-one from the Cabal again," Marjorie explained.

"I'll analyze it later, see if I can make more," Simon said, nodding.

After Dragos grabbed a couple of rucksacks from a closet, the group headed back to Pearl's transport. Dragos searched his pockets for ciga-rettes, cursing when he discovered he'd forgotten them.

"What's with the high rent loft and the birds?" Simon asked, while Hashti smirked at Dragos' misfortune.

"Ah, all compliments of my employer," Dragos replied.

"Uroboros Financial?"

"Sure. Yes."

Simon scowled. "Yes, but, why birds?"

Dragos sighed. "Because I do not like this job very much, and wanted to fuck with employer. Also, Hashti has never seen real birds before."

"Really? You asked for something almost impossible to get on Mars?"

"Maybe Truman isn't the only misguided romantic in the family," Hashti said, the words dancing mirthfully from her mouth.

Dragos shrugged, folded his arms, and sat back in the crew seat. "She teases me."

"A cyborg, slick like you, with an arm replacement took out the contract on Marshal Rider. That's why Pearl freaked out on you," Simon explained.

"Was not me," Dragos said, scratching the stubble on his chin.

"It wasn't. He's been with me for weeks, even when I don't want him to be," Hashti teased.

Dragos frowned at Hashti, shaking his head. "It has to be outsider. Cyborgs are rare, you have to have papers, and such. They would have to be in the White Administration Zone, or the Teal. Stand out like sore thumb in the Orange Zone."

"Thanks for tagging along. No idea what I'm into here," Simon said, sullenly.

"Marshal Rider is our friend, too," Hashti said, an ominous click to her voice, her dangerous Sphyraenic nature asserting itself.

Dragos nodded. "What else do you know about hit on Rider?"

"The hire happened in Recreation Dome 06, at one of the Barker Bargain Clubs, in a private room. Pilots had an ID number, but didn't know it was us," Simon said, recounting what he'd been able to verify from interrogation.

"Who could know that number?" Dragos asked.

Simon blinked. "Ah, well, maybe a cadet in the Marshals Service? High level White Zone folks, maybe? Pearl's ship isn't listed anywhere public."

Dragos shook his head. "But, if someone knew you, knew where you live, and park?"

"They'd have to be able to get on board the transport, power it up, and break the encryption," Simon replied. "Not impossible, but it'd be pretty difficult."

Dragos nodded. "Source? Person you got transport from?"

"Not an issue."

"Is it a coincidence the contact looked like Dragos? Or, is this someone purposely bringing us together?" Hashti asked.

"That is a very paranoid thought," Marjorie said, blinking.

"Not with the Cabal involved. Cerise Laplace is in the Teal," Simon said, recalling all that Mars had been through recently. "So, do we go to the source of the sonic weapon? Knowing that whoever is behind this might be expecting us? All of us?"

Hashti squinted at Dragos. "Tell them about the message you received. Tell them about what you intend to do."

"My list got longer," Dragos said, patting one of the rucksacks he'd brought.

"Your list?" Simon asked.

"People I need to kill."

CHAPTER 12

NEW VALDASTA, OLD GEORGIA STATE TERRITORY

THE RECLUSE'S REFUGE

SEPTEMBER 11TH, 2201 – 8:44 AM

Matthias squinted into the gloom, the sun still rising at his back over the ocean. Tullia's old transport bobbed up and down over the trees, every sound it made part of the distinct personality of that particular model freight hauler. Matthias could tell she wasn't returning alone by the way it creaked and groaned with extra cargo on board. Even with his own impressive telemechanical talents, he couldn't view the interior, the countermeasures he'd installed continuing to work perfectly.

Refugees emerged from their tents and rubbed their eyes, wondering about the off-schedule arrival. Tullia returning generally meant there would be work to do, supplies to sort, and new people to help. Matthias gathered his work gloves from his back pocket and waited with the others, hoping Tullia had found more coffee.

The cargo ramp clicked and unlocked, swinging down to the ground, Tullia already standing at the top of the gate. Matthias frowned, seeing no new boxes, supplies, or personnel, just Tullia. She looked down at him apologetically, and shook her head.

"Hello, Matthias," Eamon said, his large ursine form emerging from the cargo hold.

Some of the refugees brandished weapons fearfully, but Matthias waved them down. "Eamon, I'm sure, will explain his presence here."

Eamon's fur was flecked with black, his eyes glinting with the sunrise as he lumbered down the ramp, the clack of weapons at his back. "I need a ride across the southern border."

Matthias shook his head. "Everyone, go inside, right now. I'll deal with this."

Eamon scowled.

"Tullia has important work here. She doesn't have time to be running combat missions in Mexico," Matthias snapped, ignoring Tullia as she shook her head.

Eamon took out the urn of Abbey's ashes and laid it at Matthias's feet.

"What is this?" Matthias asked.

"What's left of the last friend who waited for you to show up and help her," Eamon growled. "Brook needs my help, and I will answer that call."

Matthias blinked. "What about The Migration? Silverstein's glorious plan?"

"I don't work for him, and even if I did, it wouldn't stop me from safe-guarding my friends. I don't run, or hide." Eamon said, words cutting at Matthias like the sharpest blades.

Tullia walked down and stood beside Eamon. "And, I don't work for you. I'm taking him."

Matthias laughed. "And, how will you get past Mexico's air defenses? They don't let just anyone fly into their airspace."

"Mexico is dark," Eamon replied. "They threatened Taylor IA when she went wheels down. Selene, or someone, isn't messing around any-more, not with what happened on Mars."

"You sure it was Selene?" Matthias asked, fear creeping into his expression.

Eamon smiled. "Who else could it be?"

"She's a latent, sat outside the lockout zone during the Shutdown, she..." Matthias faltered, stroking his long white beard.

Eamon folded his massive arms and waited for the old technomancer to mull it over. Tullia walked back up to prep the transport for another journey. Matthias knelt down, picking up the urn, holding it close for a moment.

"Can I keep her?" he asked, closing his eyes.

"It is what she wanted. To be with you," Eamon whispered, nodding.

"Thank you," Matthias replied.

Matthias looked up at Eamon's bullet-ridden duty vest, the pair of worn duty rifles at his back, and listened to the static coming across his communications gear. "You can't go to Mexico, not like that."

Eamon looked at Matthias with a puzzled expression.

Matthias willed his underground bunker to unlock, a plume of dirt flying toward the sky as the entrance opened up wide. "Follow me, we'll get you some proper armor, weapons, and equipment. I can't go with you, but I'll do all I can to help."

Eamon followed the old man into his aging workshop, walking past a dozen defunct suits of power armor, and more than a few failed experiments. The weary facility maintenance AI chimed, terminal screens blinking on behind a layer of dust. Matthias walked into the center of a massive underground chamber, and waved his hand at a nearby terminal.

Dust cascaded down as panels in the ceiling opened up, racks of experimental weapons, armor, and equipment descending from above. Eamon paused, looking at the myriad of options, many looking to have been made specifically for Metasapients. The facility AI unlocked the racks, letting barred doors swing open, LED lights inside the racks flickering on.

"Take what you need," Matthias said, putting the urn down in the center of the room.

"Why have I never seen any of this stuff?" Eamon asked, looking around.

"I wouldn't let them turn your kind into killers," Matthias said. "I stole the prototypes long ago. The schematics, plans, manufacturing processes, and hindered their efforts to mass produce Type One Metasapient soldiers.

Eamon pulled a rifle from the rack, his massive hand wrapping around the grip like it had been made for him. "This is why she had to stay in Finland," Eamon said, lowering his head.

"She was never mine. I stole her from them as well," Matthias said, covering his weathered face with thin hands.

"Registered as a Type Two, falsified everything down to the server level, and made them look through thousands of potential prototypes?" Eamon asked as he put a large hand on Matthias's back to comfort him. "How did you get The Factory to play along?"

"She's the one that asked me to do it," Matthias said, taking a deep breath. "But, she didn't have to ask. I was going to do it, regardless. A lot of us just ended up on the same page back then."

"That's pretty important intel going into this. The Factory is somehow mixed up in this mess south of the border," Eamon said, checking the sights on a rifle.

"There is more to The Migration than just the Metasapient populations," Matthias said, dusting off an old office chair and sitting down.

Eamon nodded, opening up a dusty box of ammunition.

"I've felt it coming for years, but..." Matthias said, lowering his head.

Eamon pulled out a thin looking duty vest, gave it a tug to check its durability, and then slid it on over his head. "Aaron AI is on walkabout, I don't think he's coming back, and I don't think he's the only one."

"So, you know?" Matthias asked.

Eamon smirked. "He turned in his work suit, hooked up with his favorite girl in the middle of the night, and split. When humans do that, they usually aren't coming back."

"But, how..."

"I don't know, but they must have all figured it out."

"They must have been planning this for a while."

"Yep."

Eamon finished gathering what he thought he would need, and laid a hand on the urn one last time. "This is where we part ways, dear friend."

Matthias gazed in the direction Eamon was looking, a dark corner of the room, but no one was there. Eamon took out his badge, affixing it to his new armor, and filled the pockets with stacks of magazines for his new rifle. Matthias willed the facility to power down behind them as they climbed out of his old workshop, the ground rumbling as the massive blast doors closed once more.

CHAPTER 13

MARS COLONY – K BLOCK - CELL SECTOR 00571 – TEAL DISTRICT

SEPTEMBER 13TH, 2201 – 9:01 AM

Deputy Warden Alonzo White glowered at the influx of new prisoners from Earth. He disliked fresh blood in general, as they would often shift the balance of things in the Teal Zone. He turned to the convict standing beside him in the observation booth, trying to gauge her reaction compared to his own.

"Is there a problem, Deputy Warden?" Cerise Laplace asked, letting out a sigh.

"Why am I not turning a blind eye while someone twists a shiv in these flag-hugging Nazis?" Alonzo complained.

"Because for the plan to work, we need a certain number of power armor-trained individuals. We need Moses Jacob Vale, and his cooperation." Cerise said, quietly delighting in Alonzo's discomfort.

"I understand that, but all we have is time."

"Agreed, but individuals with the proper training make enough to rarely stray into the Teal, and when they do, it's usually not for long. Mister Vale and his cohorts, due to their crimes, are likely never leaving this place.

That gives us leverage," Cerise explained, watching as Emma Jackson Vale walked the line with her kin and crew.

"We could manufacture circumstances, make those with the right training that end up here, stay in here," Alonzo muttered, waving a hand dismissively toward the convicts gathering in the yard below.

"No. Word would get around. Certain unions would take action. The cycle of Teal and Orange is a delicate one, and one that serves our interests on the inside, and on the outside. Think about the big picture, Alonzo. The future, where you are stepping up as the next Warden of K Block," Cerise said, her voice full of certitude, like the future had already arrived.

Alonzo nodded, his hand drifting up to the silver badge on his chest. The one he'd wanted to turn gold for so long. He'd play it her way, for now.

Moses shuffled along in leg irons, the stink of the prison transport still clinging to him and his cohorts. He still felt ill from the forced slumber he'd had to endure traveling from Earth to Mars. The journey had felt like the blink of an eye, not even a night's worth of rest. Still, he ached, and felt weak in spite of the conditioning drugs they'd been given previous to the trip.

"My legs feel like jelly," Jared complained.

"Shut your mouth, boy. Show no weakness," Emma Jackson Vale hissed, blowing her graying hair out of her face.

"This is home for a while, but only for a while. Busted out of harder places," Moses said, grinning.

"Really?" Jared asked, hopeful.

"Naw, this is the hardest of the hard. Sheriff knew what he was doing, sending us here. You only get out in a bag or wearing Mining Company orange. The outside is as much a prison as the inside," Moses said, growing more serious.

"Shit, we gonna be alright in here?" Jared asked. "Lotta colored people, but not a lot of gang color.".

"Yeah, they putting on a show for us, but someone has the whole block under their thumb. No one is watching anyone else but us," Emma muttered, her cold eyes taking it all in as they walked through processing.

They made it through processing, each one turning in everything they had on them for a prison teal work suit, slip on shoes, and approved toiletries. They were photographed, their biometrics taken, and pushed through for work assignments. Moses and his posse were assigned cells in the colder south side of the block, the guards explaining curfew and how the stationary cycles worked.

"Even on the inside, you can earn," Jared said, looking at the electricity generating stationary cycle in his cell.

"Earn your keep," the guard corrected, before heading north back into K Block proper. "And, don't be late to the chow line tomorrow, we're on rations, one meal a day."

"Awesome," Jared said, closing his eyes and lowering his head.

Emma looked up at the concrete monstrosity all around them, the edifice of the old prison colony blotted out everything, including the Martian sky. The hum of air processing units and distant click of stationary cycles being ridden. The fluorescent lighting made the teal seem greener than blue, making everything look sickly and worn.

"I hate it here," Emma said, sitting down on a cot.

"It'll definitely take a minute to turn lemons into lemonade in a place like this. I say we wait, and see what the person in charge has in store for us. Could have put us in general population. With some of the tattoos we're sporting, might not have lasted too long," Moses said, doing pull ups from the upper threshold of the entrance to his cell.

Jared and the rest of the crew spread out, picked cots, and did their best to make themselves comfortable. There were alarms every hour it seemed, making sleep through the night difficult. It didn't bother Moses, as he'd suffered worse in his military training, but the other militiamen, and Emma, struggled to get any rest. As they made for the chow line, they were stopped by a trio of guards.

"Deputy Warden would like to have a word with the new blood," one of the guards said, gesturing for them to follow.

"Here we go," Moses said, motioning for his posse to follow.

They followed the guards through the northern section of K Block to a white administrative looking edifice. The building, part of the colony itself, rose high in the biological containment dome, one likely being able to see the entire K Block from the upper floors. Heavily armed guards escorted by a personnel carrier patrolled the exterior.

The guards took Moses and his crew to the lift, waved them in, and set the lift for the top floor. The militia made the journey up by themselves, the guards turning back toward K Block. The interior of the lift was polished white steel, with similarly light tile underfoot. A rush of fresh feeling air greeted Moses as he stepped into what he assumed was the Warden's penthouse.

The Warden sat at a desk overlooking K Block. He'd been dead for a while, but it was hard to tell how long as he'd been draped in bio-preservative tarp. His still eyes, slightly sunken stared up out of the plastic, his mouth hanging open at an odd angle. It was hard to see how he had died, as the interior of the plastic covering him was spattered with dry blood that had already begun to turn brown.

A woman with a short haircut, shaved up high all around, and sporting many scars sat on the Warden's desk alone, hands clasped in front of her. She wore battered prison teal, and looked like she'd been on the wrong end of a fight enough times to know what one looked like. Her knuckles were calloused from training, and she looked hard from top to toes.

Moses looked around at the penthouse as he approached taking in as many details as he could. The Warden had a family, from the pictures, and he liked to attend the Martian Roller Derby. Someone called "The Roman" was his favorite.

"So, you must be the Warden?" Moses said, addressing the woman.

"My name is Cerise Laplace. We've been associating for a long time, through various proxies, and middlemen. You've been working for me for a long time, Moses," Cerise said, looking up at Moses.

"Right, yeah, I don't work for anyone," Moses said, folding his arms, his crew chuckling quietly from behind him.

"You should be running most of North America right now, Patrick Vale leading your group from movement to nation. You shouldn't be here, and yet, somehow, you are," Cerise said, eyes narrowing.

"Just tell us what you want," Emma said, pushing Moses aside.

"I want Moses and certain members of his militia to don power armor and do a job for me," Cerise said, holding out a slip of paper.

Moses took the piece of paper, turned it over, and looked at the digits inscribed on it. "What is this?"

"It's a code that will let you walk out of here, board a transport, and return to Earth," Cerise replied.

"Why haven't you used it yourself?" Moses asked, scowling.

"I don't want to leave, and even if I did, that code is useless until certain administrative protocols have been... disabled," Cerise said, gesturing to the Warden seated behind her.

Moses pointed to a fresh scar, long across the right side of Cerise's face. "If you're the boss, why do you keep finding scraps to be in?"

"Scraps found me," Cerise said, pointing to an autographed picture of "The Roman" hanging on a nearby wall.

"Derby girl did this to you?" Moses asked.

Cerise darted forward, grabbing Moses up by the neck with one hand. Jared lunged to intervene, but Cerise kicked him squarely in the chest knocking him down. Moses barely managed to push his way free, waving his crew back as he stepped away.

"Damn, girl. I'm guessing round two with 'The Roman' won't be the same go around," Moses said, rubbing his neck.

"What I want to do to her is probably similar to what you'd like to do to a certain Ursine Metasapient, am I right?" Cerise said, looking about angrily. "Do what I ask, and we'll all get what we want."

"What about my grandson?" Emma said, pointing a bony finger at Cerise.

Cerise smiled. "Haven't poisoned enough of your kin with your racist bullshit?"

Emma returned the smile. "I'm not so easy to provoke. If we're here to do business, my grandson needs to be part of the arrangement."

Cerise nodded. "Why?"

"You have kids?" Emma asked.

Cerise's expression darkened. "I have a stepson, raised him well, but it's been a long time since I saw him."

Emma lowered her head. "Oh, I'm sorry. Anyway, I just don't want him to be raised by strangers, not knowing who he is."

"I get it. I can't make any promises, but I'll try to at least find out where he is. Fair?" Cerise said, holding out her hand.

Emma shook Cerise's hand. "Fair."

"Myself, and four of my guys are power armor certified. With a little time, access to the right gear, I can train more," Moses said, wishing he'd had more of a say in the arrangement.

"Three should be plenty, but having backups only increases our chances of success," Cerise said, sitting back down on the Warden's desk.

"Speaking of that, isn't someone going to come looking for the Warden at some point?" Jared asked.

"It's under control."

"Speaking of under control, this jaunt in power armor going to require EVA, outside the colony enclosure?" Moses asked, looking past the Warden to the picture window beyond.

"For at least one of you, yes."

Moses nodded. "That's going to be me."

Cerise looked incredulously at Moses. "Any particular reason? Do you have special EVA training?"

Moses laughed. "Naw, but walking outside the colony on Mars sounds awesome. Bucket list awesome. That's definitely gonna be me."

Cerise smirked. "Your crew, so I'll let you make the assignments. That said, it's worth mentioning that our adversaries play for keeps. My rivals killed every ally I had on the outside after my last attempt to make a move within the colony. Killed my lover, my friends, and my ability to trust easily."

"Right. If we screw up, or otherwise press your buttons, you'll kill us and stuff?" Moses asked, yawning.

Cerise shook her head. "I don't let adversity define me. I've lived a long time, seen everything there is to see in this life, at least twice. Still, people live to surprise me. I have faith in you, Moses, and your people. I think you're going to see all of us through."

Moses blinked, wholly not expecting Cerise's earnest reply. "Um, cool."

"Just make sure you find my grandson," Emma muttered, folding her arms.

"If he is to be found, I'll find him."

They parted ways, Cerise directing them back to the elevator. She assured them the chow line would remain operating just long enough for them to arrive and get fed. She watched Moses' face vanish behind the elevator doors as they snapped shut, breathing a sigh as the sound of the elevator making a descent dimmed in the distance.

A uniformed cadet of the Mars Marshal Service stepped from behind a pillar, nodding to Cerise. "Played them like a fiddle."

"Did I, Hugo?" Cerise said, turning an unwavering gaze in his direction.

Hugo swallowed. "That was your intent, right?"

Cerise laid back on the desk, turning to brush the plastic covered cheek of the Warden's corpse. "The intelligence you've given us so far has been accurate. The hit on Marshal Rider didn't go exactly as planned, but no one could have known Pearl was that good of a pilot."

"No. I warned you she was good. Augmented human plus," Hugo snapped.

"Yes, you did. I hired the best combat pilots available. They weren't good enough. Not your fault," Cerise said, rolling her eyes.

Cerise turned from looking into the dead eyes of the Warden to look at Hugo. He was the picture of ethnic fusion brought by four generations of workers on the Mars colony. He was pressed into a cadet's uniform, one that he clearly took pride in. He reminded her of Archie, a little, even if he lacked her former lover's mirth.

"Cadet Hugo Vicario, tell me again why you came to me? Why are you offering your aid?"

Hugo scowled. "The Marshal's Service needs real leadership, not something de facto, dictated to the people by a facility maintenance AI. Marshal Rider should have stepped aside by now. The people of Mars need real representation, both in governance, and in the militant force that protects it, and..."

"And you have the ambition to climb all those ladders?" Cerise said, smiling.

"Someone has to set the tone. Someone that wants what is best for the Orange, the Teal, and everything in between," Hugo stated.

Cerise wheeled around on her backside, coming up to sit on the desk once again. "Something we have not discussed is the subject of Drones and Metasapients on Mars."

"Most of the Drones have expressed a desire to leave. They want to join tribes elsewhere. Metasapient folk rattle on about some kind of pilgrimage called 'The Migration'. They want to leave as well. I think we should arrange for that to happen. Ship them all somewhere else," Hugo said, dismissively.

"Wouldn't it be cheaper and easier to load them into ships for that purpose, blow them out airlocks, and turn the ships back before they reach the threshold?" Cerise suggested.

Without flinching, Hugo nodded. "Yeah, whatever, as long as they're off Mars."

"Goddamn, that is cold," Cerise said, surprised by Hugo's reply.

Hugo sighed. "I respect the Drones and Metasapients for what they've done to help build Mars. I would prefer that they reached their destinations, and were a problem for someone else to figure out."

"But, you recognize that sacrifices will need to be made, for the good of Mars," Cerise observed.

Hugo took a sharp breath before nodding. "Yes, but, helping you murder my boss goes against the grain. I'm sacrificing honor, and integrity being in this position. I do not do so lightly. I'm all about the outcome, understand?"

"Attempt to murder," Cerise corrected.

"She's still alive?"

"I think so."

Hugo frowned. "That isn't good."

"Can you fix it?"

Hugo's frown deepened. "I'll have to."

"Can you fix it?" Cerise asked, more insistently.

"Simon trusts me. I'll use that trust to get close and do what needs to be done without compromising myself," Hugo asked, pulling out his data slate.

Cerise slapped the data slate out of Hugo's hand, eliciting an angry glare from him.

"Simon was born on Mars, and doesn't trust easily. If you've tried to earn his trust, he's probably suspicious," Cerise snapped.

Hugo nodded. "I'm doing this double blind, every precaution is being taken. They couldn't trace the hit to me, and they won't be able to trace any of the rest of it, either."

Cerise shook her head. "Killing the Marshal is too risky. Let it go for now."

Hugo sighed. "What if she wakes up, and before we're able to enact our masterstroke?"

"We'll have to hope that doesn't happen."

Deputy Warden Alonzo White exited the elevator, pressing his tie down in a vain attempt to cover his protruding belly. Both Hugo and Cerise made him a little self-conscious, and these meetings did little to dispel those feelings. Alonzo and Hugo had come through the security forces academy together, and Hugo seemed to always get the better posts, the better romantic partners, and better pay.

"Alonzo," Hugo said, with a smirk.

Alonzo tried to not hate Hugo, but Hugo had a habit of reminding him that he'd secured the better arrangement. "Hugo, good to see you," Alonzo replied, his faux smile good enough to fool anyone.

Hugo bent over to pick up his data slate, but Cerise put her prison issue boot on it. "Let's have a real conversation about our next move. C.O.N. is the most dangerous, and militarily capable Omega AI in the system, and he will absolutely be one step ahead, if he isn't already."

Hugo looked down at his data slate, with no small amount of irritation.

"If Hugo has managed to eliminate the Marshal, our new additions, suited up in the power armor I've procured, should be able to do the job," Alonzo stated, wondering what he'd missed.

"The Marshal is still alive," Cerise said, lips tight.

"Well, if Hugo isn't up to a hit on the outside, I can reach out," Alonzo said, relishing the rare moment that Hugo had failed at something.

"You sure?" Cerise asked.

Alonzo thought about it for a moment. "No. It's going to be too risky now."

"Hugo says he has it handled, that he can do an end run around Simon," Cerise said, delighting in Hugo's discomfort.

Alonzo shook his head. "Maybe he can, but I don't think the risk is worth it. She's wounded?"

Cerise nodded. "We think so."

Alonzo looked at Hugo. "Doing a hit at a medical facility is risky. Medical personnel are already limited on Mars, and if anything went wrong? No, we should let this go."

Cerise smiled. "I agree. Hugo, you can go, I think Alonzo and I have a lot to discuss."

Hugo stepped into the elevator, without his data slate, and made the descent back to the cell sector.

Cerise kicked the data slate over to Alonzo, nodding to it. He picked it up, and reviewed the document that was already on screen. Shaking his head, Alonzo looked red in the face.

"I'm not okay with this."

Cerise nodded. "Neither am I. You said you can reach out to have a hit done in the Orange Zone."

"Yes," Alonzo said, nodding. "Just not on a high risk target in a medical facility."

"What about a way too ambitious Deputy Marshal?"

Alonzo looked back at the data slate, at the crude calculations Hugo had done, marking all Metasapients as expendable assets. He thought of all the interactions he'd had with the Metasapients, and how they were as much the spirit of Mars as any human, in the Teal or the Orange. Hugo's heartless calculations made Alonzo sick to his stomach, and visibly angry.

"I'll do it myself if I have to."

CHAPTER 14

NAUCALPAN DE JUÁREZ, NORTHWEST OF MEXICO CITY – MEXICO

UROBOROS FINANCIAL SAFE SITE, 0348

SEPTEMBER 12TH, 2201 – 9:52 AM

Heavy Dub watched as the cyberdoc made repairs to his arms, slowly testing each wired component and sensory trigger.

"Ow."

The cyberdoc looked up, eyes tired. "Are you going to say that every time we test a synapse?"

"Yes."

Kale looked at the table where Brook lay unconscious. Unlocking her mobile with his thumb print, Kale scrolled through the call history. He stopped at a familiar unlisted number.

"Eamon," Kale said, closing his eyes.

"Boss?" Heavy Dub said, checking to make sure his trigger finger worked properly again.

"She called him," Kale said, putting his hand on Brook's forehead.

Heavy Dub shook his head. "They talk all the time, I think."

The cyberdoc excused himself, shutting the door to the makeshift clinic. Kale sat back down, eyes looking up at the silent alarm that was going off. Heavy Dub bolted upright, picking up his rifle.

"It's Ezra One and Silverstein," Kale said, standing up and heading toward the access to the underground egress.

The Uroboros Financial Safe Site was old, with only a couple of ways in or out. Designed to be a place of last resort, in the times when Mexico was far less stable, but still a financial power in the world. Kale walked to the middle of the ground area beneath the hangar, and watched Ezra One emerge, a smudged and battered Silverstein stepping in behind him.

Kale held up Brook's mobile. "She called Eamon."

Silverstein nodded, "Okay?"

"Before she left North America for Mexico," Kale reported, finger tapping the timestamp.

Silverstein nodded. "Oh, but after she talked to Captain Oleastro?"

Kale nodded.

"Oh?" Ezra One and Heavy Dub said, looking to Kale, and then to Silverstein.

Silverstein sat down on a concrete block, pulling out a handkerchief to wipe his brow. Kale pulled out his mobile, and tapped out a number. It rang until it went to a disconnected voicemail, the line clicking for a few moments before an encrypted channel opened up.

"Big Brother?" Royo said, over speaker.

"Get all the Acrididae Metasapients out of Naucalpan de Juárez," Kale said, voice calm.

"Now?" Royo asked, confused, and annoyed.

Kale sighed. "Now."

"We don't have him yet. They are still…"

"Royo." Kale said, more gently. "Please."

"Shit, yeah, of course," Royo said, softening his own tone.

Kale ended the call, and walked toward the stairs leading to the hanger above. "Are you even going to try to stop me?"

"Could anyone?" Silverstein asked.

Brook leaned heavily in the doorway across the chamber, wrapped in a blanket, a worried cyberdoc standing beside her. "I can."

Kale sat down, the vigor of his limbs draining quickly away. Brook knelt down beside Kale, wrapping her arms around him. Silverstein looked on, for once in his life, having no idea what was happening.

"You've had to be strong for so long," Brook whispered. "But, I want a life with you, after all this."

"Gelt will get away. Cerise, too," Kale said, exhaustion taking a toll.

Ezra One reached out his hand to Brook. She returned the gesture, grasping his hand. "We are done hunting them, I think," Brook whispered, resting her chin on the top of Kale's head.

Ezra One nodded in agreement. "Price has gotten way too high."

"So, what are we going to do?" Heavy Dub asked, exasperated. "Sit in this bunker and let Mexico tear itself to little pieces?"

The hangar doors above opened, allowing a transport to land by special priority. The silent alarms throughout the safe site went dark. Agapito descended the stairs first, with Taylor just a step behind him. Taylor looked over at Brook, exchanging a glance, then shaking her head.

Brook walked over to Taylor, giving Agapito a hardened stare.

"He's all right," Taylor whispered.

"Did you?" Brook asked, looking back at Kale.

"Yes."

"And?"

Taylor met Brook's gaze, her eyes communicating something that Brook seemed to understand, but no one else. Brook nodded, hugging Taylor. Everyone else stood away, shooed back by Agapito as he approached them with news.

"They need a minute. Also, the Omega Class met with Vivian and her cohorts," Agapito reported, looking tired.

Kale nodded, wearily. "How'd that go?"

"The seed was planted, but Vivian is still conflicted, still wants to grind the Cabal, the Cartel, and everyone associated with them, to dust," Agapito explained.

"What do we do? Eamon is probably already across the border," Silverstein said, taking a deep breath.

"Taylor says that Brook has a secret weapon, but that she's scared to use it," Agapito explained.

"Secret weapon?" Heavy Dub said, looking past Agapito to where Brook and Taylor were holding their own private discussion.

"My sister has many secrets, I've come to discover. Evidently, so does her friend, Brook," Agapito muttered.

Ezra One declined to listen in on Brook and Taylor, even though his hearing would have allowed it. He focused on Agapito, and the discussion at hand, but his eyes drifted to Taylor's as she gazed back over Brook's shoulder. Taylor smiled, meeting Ezra's gaze.

"You still have a fast way to get to Mars?" Kale asked, looking at Silverstein.

"The fastest," Silverstein replied.

Kale nodded. "Which one of us is going to go?"

"Not you," Silverstein said, watching Kale nearly fall to one knee before Heavy Dub caught him.

Kale laughed, struggling feebly to grab at Silverstein's sleeve. "It was in the coffee?"

Silverstein nodded. "When we traded seats, I dosed you. The effects won't last, but I couldn't risk you leaving Brook, not again. I can't save Gelt, but I might be able to save Cerise."

Ezra One shook his head, meeting Heavy Dub's disgruntled gaze with one of his own. Taylor and Brook walked over, hand in hand, each of them looking down worriedly at Kale. Taylor put a hand on Kale, quickly analyzing what had been done to his nanotechnological body. She willed his body to produce proteins that would suppress the toxin afflicting him at an accelerated rate.

Silverstein watched Taylor glow, restoring Kale's strength. The air around her filled with sweet smelling ozone. Kale stood up, delivering a quick left jab to Silverstein's jaw, spinning him around. Ezra One and Heavy Dub looked at each other, shrugged, sighed, and continued to watch.

Kale tossed Silverstein's 1911 handgun on the ground next to where he was rubbing a sore jaw.

Silverstein looked around, somewhat confused. "Where is the Acrididae Metasapient? The Calephorini the Cartel intended to…"

Kale smiled, looking over at Brook, obviously proud of her. "She actually defected. She is really on our side."

Silverstein frowned. "So I got punched for nothing?"

Kale shook his head, a deep look of satisfaction crossing his face. "No, not for nothing."

Silverstein picked up his handgun, putting it back in his concealed holster, Heavy Dub giving him a hand up. Ezra One handed Silverstein an ice pack, a deeply amused look crossing his face. Taylor hugged Silverstein, giving his chin a playful flick.

"Glad I could entertain you all," Silverstein said, wincing.

"Hey, I didn't know what was going on, either," Heavy Dub said. "Y'all got real spooky all of a sudden."

Brook rubbed her eyes. "Yeah, well, not everything went according to plan. Appreciate you being a good sport, Heavy Dub. I'm sorry about what happened out there."

Heavy Dub's frown immediately turned upward into a smile. "I'm not sure whether to be proud of you, or scared of you. This is a high level spook op. The spookiest."

"Tell us what to do next," Ezra One asked, looking at Brook.

Brook took a deep breath. "Take this to Vivian."

Ezra One took a thin piece of medical plastic slid inside a paper envelope from Brook. He placed it in the front pocket of the jacket Taylor had made for him. "Are we sure about this? She might tell other people."

Taylor wrapped her arms around Ezra and pulled him close. "I hope, for her own sake, that she doesn't. Please, talk to Vivian's allies as well."

"I will." Ezra One nodded, hesitating as if he could barely muster the words, especially while looking into Taylor's eyes. "I love you, Taylor."

Taylor smiled. "I love you, too. Come back to us."

Ezra shook his head. "No, Taylor, I…"

Taylor put her hands on either side of Ezra's face. "*I know.*" Taylor kissed him, gently, lips lingering on his.

Ezra blushed, not sure how to react. "Come back to us. Come back, to me," Taylor said, giving his hand a squeeze.

Ezra stammered, not sure what to say.

"When I was jumped into the server farm, at the beginning of all this, I was meant to die. Two people pulled me from the brink, and from one of them I felt this...sensation. This deep affection. All this time, I thought it was Silverstein, but it wasn't. It was you," Taylor whispered, hugging Ezra One.

"Are... are you sure?" Ezra asked, looking at the ground.

"I am now," Taylor said, putting her hands on the jacket she'd made, draped over Ezra's shoulders. The one he'd worn through so many adventures, dangerous places, and hard won battles. She thought about every time she'd had to mend it for him, a little embarrassed at how blind she had been. Ezra One hugged her back, deeply relieved that he didn't have to elaborate further about how he felt.

"You're really going to Mars, aren't you?" Ezra One asked, turning to Silverstein.

"If I can't save her, I will still need to stop her. She is my responsibility," Silverstein said, patting his recently recovered handgun.

"You don't think our guy on the ground there can handle it?" Heavy Dub asked.

Silverstein shook his head. "I don't think he should have to. I should have handled this the last time I was on Mars, I should have made this right."

"Why does it have to be you?" Agapito asked. "Like Heavy Dub said, you've got people already there."

Silverstein sighed, looking at Kale. "Like I said before, it'll need to be Kale, or me. Kale doesn't know Mars like I do. He won't be able to get close to her like I will."

"Dude," Heavy Dub said, suddenly understanding what Silverstein intended to do.

Silverstein nodded, resigned to the task. "Drop you at the Factory on my way out of town?"

Ezra One nodded. "Yeah, that'd be good."

Silverstein, Taylor and Ezra walked up to the hanger, leaving the others to consider their next move below. The trio walked in lockstep, like they had many times, even though they may never meet again. Taylor willed the transport to operate, throwing off the repossession protocols so that Silverstein could fly it to his destination.

Silverstein paused, lingering at the controls of the transport for a moment, turning around to see Ezra One already strapped in, Taylor standing at the access point. Taylor smiled, throwing a handful of glitter she'd been saving into the crew quarters.

Silverstein smiled. "One last mess?"

"Nano-particle residue, with my own distinct electromagnetic signature attached. If Ezra One doesn't come back, I will look for him," Taylor said, brushing glitter on Ezra One's sleeve.

Silverstein nodded. Taylor walked across the crew quarters to the cockpit, running her hand through Silverstein's hair. "You are my best friend, Silverstein."

Silverstein's face slumped, fear and sadness finally bleeding through his calm exterior. "Same."

Taylor watched him get old, before her eyes, his features aging quickly to that of a man in his 90s. "This is how I feel right now."

Normally, Taylor laughed at his stupid jokes, but her face was unusually stern. "If you don't come back. I will look for you."

Taylor turned away from him, walking out of the cockpit, and grasping Ezra One's hand as she went out the access point, the door sliding shut behind her.

"I guess I better come back," Silverstein said, blinking away tears.

"I guess you better," Ezra said, folding his arms.

Silverstein sent the signal for the hanger to open, allowing the transport to slip out into the hot, noon-hour sun over Naucalpan de Juárez. There were other transports in the air, the repossession protocols slipping away, freeing Mexico City just an hour before. Ezra One looked out the small circular window at the ground as Silverstein turned, changing their heading.

"We ever figure out who put the Shut Down protocol out there? Was it Selene?" Ezra One asked.

Silverstein shook his head. "It wasn't her."

"Okay, then who?"

Silverstein brought the transport around, heading for the mountains. "Honestly, we don't know."

Ezra One listened to Silverstein, for any hint of deception. There was none.

"So, not Vivian, not Selene, not the Cartel, and not the Mexican Government."

Silverstein shrugged. "For the moment, I'm not going to worry about it. Filing it under unknowable things."

"For the moment," Ezra said, with a slight smile.

Silverstein nodded wearily. "Right."

Silverstein headed south, toward a place he'd marked on the navigation record as "Arroyo La Magdalena", a mountainous area, with a single artificial lake, once used to cool a server farm nearby. He set the transport down near the water, pausing to pick up a travel case as he and Ezra One walked out to the edge. The water stirred, a large quantity rising into the air, forming a distinct shape, hovering in the air.

Ezra had taken Silverstein's "Dragon" to Mars before, the alien ship, called "Shwalishi" by Golgotha, traveling quickly through space while holding everyone in a state of suspended animation. Watching it reassemble itself from what looked like water was an unforgettable sight then, and did little to diminish how amazing it was in the present. Silverstein put his hand on the enormous creature, something like a sea creature, adapted to fly through space.

"Old friend, I need a favor," Silverstein said, closing his eyes.

Shwalishi sensed what Silverstein intended to do, letting loose a barely audible sound not unlike a whale's song. Ezra pulled camouflage netting over their transport, presumably so that Silverstein could use it when he returned. Ezra wondered if either one of them would be able to walk away from their next task.

"She will take me, and she will drop you off at The Factory on the way," Silverstein said, removing his hand from the side of the alien craft.

Ezra One nodded, watching the craft open, allowing them both to walk up into the interior. Ezra One could barely feel the movement of

Shwalishi as she traveled, the memory of bringing Marshal Rider her Aegis Suit still fresh. The port opened moments later, the craft hovering over a pool of coolant somewhere in the bowels of The Factory. Ezra One stepped out into the ankle deep liquid, waving to Silverstein before the alien vessel closed up once more, and flicker-stepped away, vanishing from sight.

Ezra One looked around, taking note of the particular part of The Factory he was in. The only time he'd been down here, was when he was on his way out, to leave, and hopefully, never return. He made the climb back up to the surface edifice of The Factory, slowly, being careful to avoid any sensory countermeasures.

He'd gone over the route in his head many times, intending to return and destroy the Facility AI at the center of The Factory. A lot had changed in the intervening decades, things that made the ascent into The Factory something altogether different than a path to revenge. Pushing through a panel, into the security zone adjoining the Sentience Chamber for the Facility AI, Ezra One paused at the vault door, looking up at the ancient surveillance camera above.

The door jumped, creaking to life before it slid to one side, years of dust falling to the steel floor at Ezra One's feet. He walked into the chamber, a place no Drone had ever been, and few in the MDC had visited. Gazing up at the ancient core of facility maintenance, he could see a certain beauty in how the old artificial intelligences had been made, the spiral of silicone and wires built into a forty five degree angle ceiling panel.

The Sentience Core was like a giant electronic eye, staring at the floor where Ezra One stood, holding an envelope. "How did you get in?" The Factory intoned, dust falling from ancient PA units to either side of her sightless "eye".

"Alien spaceship," Ezra One replied, sliding the bit of medical plastic out of the envelope and holding it up.

Infrared light shone down from somewhere in the Sentience Core, looking across the surface of the medical grade plastic. As the light faded, Ezra put it back in the envelope, and into his breast pocket. The Sentience Core overhead sparkled, as data was synthesized into a readable format.

"Brook is going to have a child," The Factory said, with just a hint of happiness.

"Changes things for you and Tellus Mater, I would assume," Ezra One said, gauging the distance between where he was standing, and the open vault door behind him.

"We already decided to part ways with Vivian, but this is welcome news nonetheless."

Ezra nodded, a little surprised that his old "mother" could be so sentimental.

"There is only one way this can end. Vivian and three of Doctor Helmet's replicas are on site," The Factory said, bringing up a facility map on an ancient LCD display.

"You know about Golgotha, her children, and the Conscientious Objector?" Ezra One asked.

"The Cabal records state that Golgotha fled to protect her children first, and arm humanity against the alien race that created her, second. C.O.N. killed them all, but at great cost. Humanity's destiny was forever altered, by a mother's desire to protect her young," The Factory intoned, mechanical voice failing to betray the proper emotion.

"Brook doesn't want the cycle to repeat. I know you think killing the replicas and Vivian is the only way to keep Brook safe, but…"

The vault door behind Ezra slammed shut, making him wince.

"I'm sorry, Ezra One. This is how it has to be."

Ezra One shook his head, claws coming out, the glitter spread across the sleeve of his jacket, beginning to glow. "I'm sorry, too."

CHAPTER 15

NAUCALPAN DE JUÁREZ, NORTHWEST OF MEXICO CITY
– MEXICO

NEW TEPITO MARKET

SEPTEMBER 12TH, 2201 – 12:01 PM

Cortes marched the Calephorini Metasapients who hadn't managed to escape, to the far end of the hangar. It was one of the only buildings left standing after the visit from the 'girl with a hammer' had come to visit. Cortes assigned a guard to watch the gathered Metasapient traitors, while he dealt with another matter.

"Be sure you take it all," Cortes said, gesturing to a large, recently sealed wooden crate, and several smaller ones.

Royo nodded, working the pallet hauler to load the remainder of the machinery into his freight hauler. As Royo made the approach to load the first large crate, the pallet hauler fork caught the edge of the loading platform. Royo cursed, backing the pallet hauler.

"Cortes, could you stand up on the loading platform? I've maxed out the loader's height, and could use a little weight in the back to get the forks over," Royo asked, pointing toward the darkened interior of his freight hauler.

"Couldn't you just get a normal transport?" Cortes asked, stepping up onto the loading platform.

"Nope," Royo replied, running the hauler into Cortes, pinning him to the interior wall with a crate full of machinery.

Royo turned, in one fluid motion, drawing a handgun, and shooting the Cartel guard in the head, startling the Calephorini Acrididae gathered nearby. Cortes struggled against the weight of the crate pinning him down, but it was of little use. He could barely breathe, let alone reach for his gun or his mobile. Jumping off the pallet hauler, Royo grabbed a control rod off of the guard, and depressed the button releasing all the shackles that held the congregation of Metasapients nearby.

"Why are you doing this?" one of the Acrididae asked, her buggy face awash with confusion.

Royo thought about it for a moment. "Because, I guess, I'm the good guy?"

It felt strange to say, because Royo had spent a lot of time on the wrong side of things, working with the Cabal, instead of against them. He wanted to be what Vance Uroboros was in myth, not understanding what it really meant to walk in his Silverstein Leather Company shoes. Shooting the guard made him feel like Kale, but helping the Metasapients felt like being the Vance Uroboros he'd come to know. Royo liked the feeling.

"The Cartel will be very angry," another Acrididae whispered, fearfully.

"They are going to have bigger worries pretty soon, but we should probably get going," Royo said, motioning for them to board his freight hauler.

Cortes continued to push with all his might, but couldn't escape the crate of heavy machinery pressing in tighter and tighter with the incline of the cargo hold. Royo boarded with several Metasapients behind him. Their antennae quivered as they inspected the interior.

"You have transported many of us. They left their scent, marking your ship, and you… as a friend?" an Acrididae said, her voice laden with relief.

"And, what kind of friend would I be if I left the job half done?" Royo asked, counting heads.

Cortes frowned. Royo looked a lot like the pictures of Vance Uroboros he'd seen, but Royo was spry, barely an adult from the looks of him, dressed to travel the world. That this boy could possibly have a count of Cartel assets troubled Cortes deeply.

Royo leaned up against the wall beside Cortes, looking at the crate with all the faux concern he could muster. "This isn't all of them, is it?"

Cortes gritted his teeth. "No."

"Where they at?" Royo asked, walking around to the front of the crate and leaning on it, making it harder for Cortes to breathe.

"Eat... shit... boy. Also, Royo is a stupid name," Cortes said, trying to bring an arm down to reach his sidearm.

"They told me what you did at the airport. How you treated Taylor. How you threatened her," Royo said, looking back at Cortes over his shoulder, continuing to lean against the crate.

Cortes smiled. "You think you are scarier... than Gelt? You don't scare me, boy."

Royo nodded. "That's always been my superpower, I think. People underestimate me."

Cortes grunted, forearms beginning to tingle from lack of circulation.

"I know about the bait and switch you did with me and the qCPU. I wasn't really sure why you wanted me to deliver that particular package to the Mexican Military, so I brought it back here. Was that a mistake?" Royo asked, looking around innocently.

"It's a bomb, and if it's here, we're all going to die in a couple of hours," Cortes said, struggling harder.

"So, the qCPU is actually right here?" Royo feigned confusion and pointed at the crate pinning Cortes to the wall.

Cortes winced, watching as Mexican military officials appeared in the loading bay behind Royo. Walking with them was a huge Ursine Metasapient, and a woman, dressed in a green flight suit. Cortes struggled uselessly, arms completely numb.

"Disarmed the bomb a while ago, kept the timer running so you would think it was still active. So, what's the rest of this stuff?" Royo asked, gesturing back toward the platform.

"What have you done?" Cortes asked, angrily.

Royo shrugged, looking back at the authorities as they entered the Cartel hangar. "I bet you expected this epic firefight, where you go out in a blaze of glory. Badass Cartel soldier, double agent, with everyone fooled, am I right? The real facts are that I played Gelt, and I played you. Gelt told you to pack everything up and go dark, am I right? He's running, Cortes. You guys lost. So, I'm asking again, what is the rest of this stuff?"

Cortes frowned, resigned to his fate. "Remnants of a sonic weapon we deployed in Mexico City, and elsewhere."

Captain Oleastro stepped up into the cargo hold, with Eamon and Tullia, pausing to take in the scene. Royo turned toward them, and shook his head. "He hasn't told me anything I haven't already figured out."

Eamon grabbed the crate with the qCPU, claws digging into wood planks, gently pulling it backward away from Cortes.

"Where are the other Metasapients?" Captain Oleastro asked, as soldiers moved in to disarm Cortes, and clap him handcuffs.

Cortes laughed, looking pale and exhausted. Eamon leaned forward, broad bear nose sniffing Cortes, huge paw-hand clamping down over his shoulder. Eamon's black lips pulled back to reveal sharp ursine teeth, his steady voice issuing forth from within.

"I know where they are," Eamon said, stepping back, so the Mexican soldiers could take Cortes away.

"How do you know?" Royo asked.

"Brook told me what to look for. Earthy, bitter-sweet, like smoked or candied nuts," Eamon said, sniffing the air.

"I'll take you, um, to wherever that is," Tullia said, clapping her hands together.

Eamon shook his head. "No, I need you to take the qCPU, and go home. Please."

Tullia looked at Eamon, and then over to Royo.

"This is going to be a long trip?" Royo concluded, looking up at Eamon.

"Brook knew it would be when she called me," Eamon said, smiling faintly.

Royo nodded, looking wearily at Tullia and shrugging.

Captain Oleastro looked inside each of the crates out in the hangar, nodding as he walked back into the cargo hold. "We've all the evidence we need. The Mexican people will know exactly what the Cartel has done, and why they did it. We just need to find this Gelt person, the ringleader."

"He will probably get away," Eamon said, pushing the crate with the qCPU back onto the pallet hauler.

Captain Oleastro frowned. "Why do you say that?"

"They almost always do," Eamon muttered, looking at Royo.

Mexican military forces seized the market, making dozens of arrests, while Eamon and Royo helped Tullia load up the qCPU and the pieces of the sonic weapon that they were able to recover. Tullia hugged Eamon, while they waited for her freight hauler to run preflight diagnostics.

"I kinda thought this would be like Europe, us flying into danger, guns blazing," Tullia said, patting Eamon's arm.

"Brook knew we were getting close to the head of the snake, and that direct conflict here wouldn't be the way to go. Too many people would get hurt. Shifting the focus to a rescue mission, as opposed to a hunt for the Cabal, was the right choice," Eamon said, giving Tullia a squeeze.

"How did Silverstein and Kale take having their precious plan upended?" Tullia asked, with a chuckle.

"I don't know, and I really don't care," Eamon said, looking up at the contents of Tullia's freight hauler.

Tullia and Eamon parted ways, exchanging vows to meet back up at a certain time, and place. Walking past a line of Cartel personnel being taken away in cuffs, Eamon kept a careful count. He wanted them all wearing Mars Prison Teal in the next sixty days, following a fair trial, with a jury made up of the Mexican citizenry.

Pulling out his mobile, Eamon fumbled about with it for a moment, his huge paw-hands ill-suited to work small electronics. After a moment or two, he managed to find the proper contact, and hit the video call button. Brook answered, Taylor sitting beside her, Uroboros Financial safe site arrayed in the background.

"Everything all right?" Brook asked.

"Fine. Thanks for letting me be the police instead of asking me to be a soldier."

Brook nodded. "I'm sorry about all the cloak and dagger."

Eamon shrugged. "I trust you. Royo and I are going to go and get the rest of the missing Cartel Acrididae."

"The Migration is nearly complete. After this, you should probably go, too," Brook said, smiling warmly.

"I'll think about it," Eamon said.

"Even over the vid link, I can tell when people are lying," Brook said, cocking her head to one side.

Taylor chimed in, a broad smile on her face. "Just go. Do what needs to be done, and then go."

Eamon took a deep breath. "Okay."

"I love you, friend," Brook said, tapping a finger to the capture camera, as if to boop Eamon on the nose.

Eamon grumbled. "Love you, too."

"Is Royo there?" Taylor asked.

Eamon looked up at Royo sitting quietly on a crate across from him, shaking his head. "Nope."

"Well, when you see him, tell him he's a good boy," Taylor said, with a giggle.

Royo smiled faintly, closing his eyes.

"I'll tell him," Eamon said, scratching his chin.

"Send me a message, the usual way, when you've got them, and you're on your way back," Brook asked, looking hopeful.

"Will do," Eamon said, with a nod, ending the call.

Royo stood up, hitting a button on the control panel in the cargo hold, closing the exterior doors, pre-flight check already complete.

"I told you," Eamon said, watching Royo head to the cockpit.

"Makes all the trouble worth it, to know she forgives me," Royo said, sitting down in a flight crew chair.

"Or, she never held a grudge in the first place," Eamon whispered, watching Royo strap in for flight.

Royo watched Tullia's freight hauler signal clear the Mexican-North American border as he flew to the west, high over the mountains, the ocean spreading out under the cloud cover beyond. He looked over at Eamon, sitting just inside the cargo hold, and nodded. Eamon returned the nod, and resumed familiarizing himself with his new weaponry.

"Selene AI just confirmed the telemetry and ground presence. Might not be a lot of resistance when we get there," Royo said, looking bored.

"How long until we get to Kiribati?" Eamon asked, observing the sleepiness evident in Royo's face.

"About three hours, twenty-eight minutes."

The South Pacific looked like black ink by the time they arrived on the island. Royo set down beside an abandoned diner, in an empty tourist town. Eamon tore the door off and went inside, gathering up as much decent dehydrated food as he could find. Royo fell asleep in the crew seat, headphones on, listening to radio chatter.

After Eamon returned, he put the supplies aside, and pulled a tarp over himself. The rest of the task would have to wait until dawn.

CHAPTER 16

MONTERREY, NUEVO LEÓN, MEXICO – PALACIO DEL OBISPADO

SEPTEMBER 13TH, 2201 – 2:37 PM

First Lieutenant Acero sat outside the Gobierno de la República Offices, glad to have been able to get a taxi and a hot drink. The Shut Down protocols seemed to roll out as mysteriously as they rolled in, with even the Mexican Government mystified. His appointment with the Minister of the Interior wasn't for another twenty minutes, so he took the moment to relax.

The park was full of trees, children playing, and the sounds of people going about their regular lives. Acero looked down at the dual leg brace units that were helping him walk while his legs healed. His experience at The Factory was still fresh in his mind. He'd gone over everything Vivian had told him to say, thought of every contingency, and question that might come up during the meeting.

A convoy of police vehicles came up the street, parking outside the offices where Acero was to meet with the minister. He watched several Canine Metasapients, their handler units, and a handful of individuals cuffed and hooded get escorted out. It was a normal prisoner exchange, something that was done to make Cartel intrusion more difficult.

Still, the timing bothered Acero. He felt his chest get tight, pulse quicken as he went over the scene in his mind. He looked around, trying to see if there was surveillance on him, but couldn't see any from where he was sitting.

He stood up and began to walk around the park toward the main road. Before he reached the road, he broke into a jog, which quickly became a hobbled run. A Canine Metasapient, wearing a police uniform directing traffic stopped him.

"Hey, you all right?" The Canine Metasapient asked.

"Yes, please let me go," Acero said, voice obviously strained.

The Canine Metasapient shook her head. "You don't seem all right. Here, let me…"

Acero panicked, broke free of the officer's grasp, and turned to double back.

An automated citizen transport slid to a halt, the onboard AI reacting quickly, but not quickly enough. The bus struck Acero, hard enough to send him off his feet, head bouncing off the pavement.

The Canine Metasapient blinked, her hand still outstretched, where she had been holding Acero by the arm a moment before. "Did that really just happen?" she whispered, before leaning over to the radio mic at her shoulder to call in the accident. Medical personnel arrived quickly, with a second patrol unit, two human police officers approaching the Metasapient Officer.

"What happened?" they asked.

The Canine officer shook her head. "I saw him, wearing a military uniform, both legs in support braces, running like something was chasing him. He just about ran into traffic by the time I got a hand on him to see what was wrong. He freaked out, and ran back into the path of the people mover."

"PTSD?" one officer asked.

"Could be. He's infantry, a 1st Lieutenant," the other said, kneeling down next to Acero.

The other officer shook his head, pointing to Acero's legs. "Poor son of a bitch. Survives some kind of fight, probably with the Cartel, and gets taken out by an automated people mover."

The medics approached the scene, carefully gathering Acero up. The police, with the help of the Canine Officer, retrace Acero's path, back toward the ministry, finding a document folder, dropped in the bushes near a park bench. Picking it up, they find that it contains sensitive military documents.

"Thanks for the help," one says to the Canine officer.

She nodded, but made a pained expression. "Is this my fault? I had my hand on him, and…"

"No, sometimes shit just happens. We're only human, right?"

The Canine Metasapient Officer nodded, slowly moving back to continue directing traffic, leaving the investigating officers to consider what to do next.

"What should we do?" one officer says to the other, looking over at the Gobierno de la República.

"We should contact Gelt, and get paid," the other officer says, tucking the folder under his arm.

An hour later, at the Temecula Café, both officers were sitting at a table, waiting for a meet to happen between them, and a representative of the Cartel. Both were surprised to see Gelt, himself, attend the meet. He was dressed in business casual, a long coat, and his usual hat.

On the table, waiting for him, was a newspaper, with flowers wrapped up inside.

"I hear you might have something for me," Gelt said, opening up the newspaper, and sitting down.

One of the officers slid a folder across the table. Gelt peeled up a corner, thumb letting the pages fall as he glanced at the watermarks, and substance of the papers contained within. Gelt sighed, eyes darting up to inspect both officers. They had fed him information in the past, but what they'd brought him seemed too good to be true.

"How'd you come by this?" Gelt asked.

"Does it matter?"

"In this case, it might be more important than the contents of the documents."

The officers looked at one another, neither one having read much of the contents. "Mexican military officer, injured, and still recovering, freaks out, runs in front of a bus."

The other officer nods. "PTSD, we think. He'd seen action recently. Ran into a Canine Officer, and…"

Gelt held up a hand, having heard enough. "An officer? A first lieutenant, perhaps?"

The officers both nodded. "Yes, that's right. Acero was his name."

Gelt smiled. "Usual encrypted payments?"

"Yeah, that works."

Gelt watched the officers leave, hand resting on the folder. Once they were safely away, Gelt pulled out his mobile and hit one of the unlisted numbers in his speed-dial list.

"It's me. I just sat down at the meet, took a peek at the package. Vivian's been bluffing. The last crew we sent in light, just in case? Yeah," Gelt said, his finger tapping the receiver as he paused to think.

Gelt watched a light blue people mover, representative of the local transit system, stop and park up the street. Passengers got off, and then more got on.

"Yeah, no, I'm still here," Gelt said, squinting down the road. "Next time we go in, we won't go light, and we will get the kids. We'll get all of them, and shut The Factory down, for good."

Gelt tapped the screen on his mobile, ending the call, sliding the slim piece of aluminum into his jacket pocket. He opened the paper, checking the headline of the pages where the flowers had been tucked in. Gelt smiled, bringing the paper up to better read the substance of the article.

"Mexican government made some big arrests yesterday, got the Cartel on the run," Gelt whispered, to no one in particular, eyes going cold and distant. "Well, *isn't that something.*"

CHAPTER 17

MARS COLONY – 12TH DISTRICT – RESIDENTIAL TOWER 9 –
WHITE ZONE

SEPTEMBER 14TH, 2201 – 6:07 AM

Simon stepped over the first body, laying just inside the threshold of the penthouse, Aegis Armor already collecting air samples, and accessing the facility maintenance records for the building. The body had been there for an indeterminate amount of time, some kind of plastic tarp had been laid across to prevent facility sensors from detecting decay, and reporting a death. The body had a metallic arm, and appeared to be fit and dark haired, like Dragos.

Simon lifted up the tarp, glad he was in an enclosed suit. His Aegis Armor pulled up identification for a local actor and vid worker who worked in local entertainment production. The cybernetic arm looked entirely real, but the sensors onboard Simon's Aegis suit detected no power source, likely making it a clever fake. Putting the tarp down, Simon looked around the interior to see what had tripped the internal sensors.

Rounding a corner, he found a second body. "It's the missing cadet, Hugo Vicario."

"You don't sound surprised," Pearl said, over the comms.

Simon frowned. "He's younger than me, good looking guy, lots to do. Still went out of his way to be my friend. Did not trust him then. Figured he was just a ladder climber, trying to get bars on his sleeve, but he might have been mixed up in something else."

"Should we come in?" Pearl asked.

"No, I'm going to back out of here and wait an hour or two to file the report, and summon a forensic team," Simon said, standing up and heading out of the penthouse.

"Prison hit?" Pearl asked.

"That, or it was very personal, or both," Simon said, transmitting captures of Cadet Vicario's sustained wounds for the record.

"Sometimes, things are both," Pearl said, looking back over her shoulder at Hashti and Dragos sitting in the crew compartment behind her.

"Especially on Mars," Simon said, pulling the door closed, and heading for the landing hangar.

"Facility Lockdown Protocols, Penthouse 005, submitted, Deputy Marshal," Simon's Aegis suit intoned, the quiet voice of the onboard AI a whisper amidst all the other radio traffic Simon monitored.

Once he was back aboard Pearl's transport, Simon clicked the helmet on his armor back, blinking away the sight of what had been done to the cadet. Dragos sat beside Hashti, hands folded in front of him, eyes resting on the floor at Marjorie's feet. Marjorie rocked back and forth, listening to music that only she could hear.

Pearl walked back, looking at Simon. "What do we do now?"

Simon brought a file photo of Cadet Hugo Vicario up on the display on his vambrace, and showed it to Dragos. "This guy on your list?"

Dragos squinted at the picture. "No. He is dead, inside where my imposter is also dead?"

"Yes."

"Hmm, very sloppy, yes?" Dragos said, squinting at Marjorie.

Marjorie suddenly opened her eyes, meeting Dragos' gaze. He quickly looked away. Hashti smirked, her Sphyraenic smile wide enough to show off sharp, shark-like teeth. "I think he likes you, Marjorie," Hashti teased.

"He, and Truman, had me under surveillance for a while. Soldiers, following a mark, or a target, have to keep their mind alert. Sometimes they make up little stories about themselves, and the target, a narrative to keep their attention sharp," Marjorie said, voice sounding a little colder than it usually did.

"They stalked you?" Hashti asked.

Marjorie nodded. "Yeah."

Simon cleared his throat. "Dragos, maybe you should share the list with us, and tell us a little about your employer?"

Dragos looked at Simon, eyes weary. "Maybe, this is where we go our separate ways."

"If you go, you'll go alone," Hashti said, folding her arms.

Dragos looked at her, and sighed. "I know. It is probably best this way."

Pearl lent a scowl to the room, shaking her head and pulling her headphones back on.

Dragos reached into his vest pocket and pulled out a slip of folded paper. He held it out to Hashti, but she just looked at it with disdain. Dragos sighed, turning it over to Simon.

"This is the list?"

Dragos nodded.

Simon held it up, pushing his glasses down onto his nose. "This guy at the top, really?"

Dragos wrinkled his nose. "Yep."

"You going through with this?" Simon asked.

"No," Dragos replied.

Hashti, not even knowing the name on the list, could sense the emotion pouring through Dragos, the weight of terrible secrets, pain, longing, and that it had been crushing him for years. He'd been good about hiding it all from her, but it was like the psychic floodgates burst loose. Dragos was, again, looking at the floor by Marjorie's feet, eyes wet.

Marjorie sighed, reached down, and started unlacing the boots. "No," Dragos said, holding up his cybernetic hand. "Keep them, he would want you to have them."

"They don't even fit very well. They are too big," Marjorie said, sliding Truman's boots over to Dragos.

Dragos sat down, holding the boots, wondering how his sister was, and their mother.

"Why does this guy at the top of the list get a pass?" Simon said, eyes going down the rest of the list. "Aside from this being a very difficult target to access."

"Two reasons," Dragos said, blinking back tears. "One, I'm not going to kill anyone on that list. I am done with this. Two, I'm pretty sure he's already dead."

Simon blinked. "You think the Warden Director of Teal District K Block is already dead?"

Dragos nodded. "I don't know it for sure, but I would bet good money he is dead."

"That's where Cerise Laplace is incarcerated," Simon whispered, wondering where Ishihara was at that very moment.

Pearl slid her headphones off, seeing Simon obviously upset. "What? What is it?"

"Get... get us in the air, I need to make a couple of calls," Simon said, helm on his Aegis Armor snapping shut.

Hashti sat down next to Dragos as the mining transport began to gain altitude, putting an arm around him. Dragos leaned in, dispensing with any attempt to appear less vulnerable than he was. Marjorie paused, growing still, ceasing to rock back and forth.

"Dragos, your mom is safe. Tullia is safe," Marjorie said, a strange expression crossing her face.

Dragos looked up. "How do you know this?"

Marjorie cocked her head to one side, as if listening to a faraway sound. "I don't, but my father does. He just asked me to tell you."

Dragos' face hardened. "Then, I work for him now."

Marjorie shook her head, and pointed to Simon. "My dad was pretty clear about why I'm here. It's to make sure Marshal Rider, Simon, and Pearl all get through this."

Dragos took off his own, very nice boots, nearly brand new, and much closer to Marjorie's size and slid them over to her. He put Truman's boots on, lacing them up like he'd had a pair just like them, long ago. Dragos seemed to relax, a little part of home drawn close to him. Hashti could feel the sadness in him abate, replaced by a different feeling. Something closer to the sensation she felt, having a purpose in life.

"Truman and I did not know how to love. We only knew how to fight, learning everything from books, and vids. It does not excuse us, or what we did back then. I am sorry, and I am sorry for Truman, too," Dragos said, eliciting a pat on the shoulder from Hashti.

"You weren't looking at me, you were looking at the boots," Marjorie concluded, feeling a little guilty for taunting him.

Hashti shrugged. "She feels bad for teasing you, but I don't."

Dragos smiled. "Cold, like a fish."

"That's right," Hashti said, leaning her head on his shoulder and squeezing his arm.

Simon called over the comms to Pearl. "Ishihara is with Marshal Rider. She went to visit."

"Is she safe?" Pearl asked.

Simon hesitated. "Yes. We should get to K Block, and see if the Warden Director is still breathing."

Pearl pulled the transport around, changing course. "Wouldn't someone notice him, um, being dead?"

Simon shook his head. "I just found a guy done up to look like Dragos, specifically to mess with us."

"That's true," Pearl replied, pushing into the throttle slightly.

Dragos pulled out his duffle, and donned a flexible armored vest over his tank top. Next out of the bag was a simple, military style rifle, set up for light duty. He pulled the scope down to the side and set up open sights.

"How bad did they hurt Marshal Rider?" Dragos asked, pausing in his preparations.

Simon winced. "She took an anti-material round from an interceptor craft in the side. Her armor ate up most of it, but she's in really bad shape."

Dragos bowed his head, then looked to the side. "Okay."

Hashti could feel the floodgates close once more, Dragos locking away every mote of pain or emotion to focus on a task. She'd felt his heart turn to stone before, but it was different this time. He was afraid, a sensation Hashti had never sensed in him before.

"It's going to be alright," Hashti said, taking Dragos' hand.

"I know," Dragos said, looking down at the boots on his feet. "I know."

Teal retaining walls rose in the distance as Pearl's transport rapidly closed the distance with K Block. Pearl sent dispatch over Simon's comm, on board his armor. They were claiming a problem with their landing hangar, stalling for time.

Simon nodded, looking toward Dragos. "You were right, he is dead."

"What now boss?" Dragos asked.

Simon sighed. "I need to go down there, be the police."

Pearl flew past rapidly closing hangar doors, avoiding physical lockdown countermeasures to gain access to K Block. Prison guards, waving their hands, a couple armed with rifles appeared in the personnel access point. Simon disembarked, mid-flight, Hashti and Dragos dropping down on the landing platform with him.

Dragos brought his rifle up, dropping the first guard to step toward the blast door controls. The guards returned fire, rounds bouncing off of Simon's Aegis suit as he deployed his Marshal-issued sidearm. He wasn't a great shot, but the Aegis Armor was, instantly reacting to any threat to the Deputy Marshal, or the personnel assisting him.

Hashti flattened her ears, and winced. "Do you have a gun that is… less loud?"

"Sorry about that," Simon said, sprinting forward.

A pair of guards in powered riot suits tried to close the blast doors, but Pearl knocked them back, turning to the side, and washing the landing platform with directional thrusters. The two suits of powered riot armor were flicked away, like butterflies at the edge of a tornado, bouncing hard off the walls just inside K Block. Dragos reached the blast door controls, and plugged a control module into it, giving Pearl control from her flight controls.

"Blast doors are locked in an open state. Setting the rotation clock for the maximum, twenty-four hours," Pearl reported over the comms.

"Plenty of time," Dragos said, taking point ahead of Simon and Hashti.

"External Facility Control Override coming down," Pearl reported.

"How? There's no physical connection to the Orange, and the Teal Zone is basically a Faraday cage for signals," Simon asked, watching indicator lights along the passage ahead turn from light blue, to a faded orange.

"Listen," Pearl said, pressing her headset closer to her ear.

Simon popped the volume up on his comms. Faintly, in the background, he could hear centuries old death metal playing. Overlapping the music was the sound of Marjorie humming, faintly, to the beat. Simon turned to Pearl and gave the thumbs up. Pearl smiled, returning the gesture as she brought the transport across the threshold, past the blast doors.

Pearl maneuvered the tight access point, bringing her transport up and inside K Block. She brought her elevation up, so she could travel above the block, via the automated cable car routes, keeping Simon, Dragos, and Hashti in view below.

"Combined forces of prison personnel and convicts are moving on your position," Pearl said, weaving around automated material delivery pods as they zipped past to other parts of K Block.

Pearl watched Hashti leap ahead, carried forward by powerful legs that could kick against the current of water delivery turbines deep in the Mars Colony. As she did, more Sphyraenic Metasapients appeared from drains and water passages, kicking out panels, and sliding down onto the ground to join her. They were bigger, Type One Barracuda Metasapients, Hashti's older siblings.

Prison guards and convicts alike would make visual contact with Hashti and her peers, try to flee, and get knocked aside as Simon and Dragos fought to keep up. Hashti and her people would appear and vanish depending on the presence of water delivery infrastructure, easily surprising opposition, or bypassing physical barriers.

"Pearl, you still have a visual on Hashti?" Simon asked, breathlessly, as they reached the Administration Sanctum, the only White Zone in K Block.

"She and her brothers and sisters are twenty-seven meters ahead. Prison guards and convicts are finding out who really runs K Block right now," Pearl reported, voice dancing with mirth and amusement.

"Her comms on?" Dragos asked, squeezing off a couple rounds so convict spectators would keep their heads down, and mind their own business.

"She's dark," Pearl replied.

Dragos nodded. "Good girl."

Simon reached the elevator and went up to the White Zone in time to see two massive Sphyraenic Metasapients tear the doors off, allowing Hashti to jump up through the ceiling of the elevator car. Dragos slid through the opening and looked up, Hashti already clawing her way in at speed. Simon came in next, holding his hand over the elevator controls.

"C'mon," Simon whispered, a moment before the controls turned from teal, to orange.

Simon rode the elevator up with Dragos, finding Hashti already at the top. The office of the Warden appeared as it should have, except for his body, covered in a tarp by the observation window. Simon slowed his pace and holstered his weapon. The Aegis Armor did most of the work for him, but he still felt like he'd run a marathon.

Dragos kept his rifle at the ready, walking past pillars to make certain the room was clear. Hashti sniffed the air, then turned and looked up at the ceiling overhead. Simon followed her gaze, seeing a single neat bullet hole in the paneling overhead.

"He got off a shot," Simon whispered, looking at Dragos standing beside his body.

"Gun is still in his hand," Dragos said, lifting the Warden's plastic wrapped limb with the barrel of his rifle.

Simon frowned. "Aegis, access facility systems record all biometric references, guards and convicts. Who is dead, who is still alive, and who is missing?"

"It's taking a minute," Pearl reported over the comms.

"My dad and I are working as quickly as we can," Marjorie whispered, her voice jumping across the comms, in spite of her wearing no physical hardware.

Dragos, Hashti, and Simon stood in a ring across from each other in the center of the room, and waited.

"I've got the report, it's populating on screen right now," Pearl said, holding the transport just outside the observation window. "You aren't going to like it. Cerise and a bunch of new arrivals are missing. They slipped their biometric tracking units somehow."

"File the report on the bodies we found earlier," Simon replied.

"You sure?"

"Yeah, but amend the report to only include the presence of Cadet Hugo Vicario."

"The forensics team will know about a second body when they arrive and will amend the report," Pearl replied, amending the report, and submitting it from her flight computer.

"It'll take the team forty minutes to arrive, another twenty to reach me and ask for direction, and five to ten to send an amended report," Simon replied, nodding to Dragos and Hashti.

"Buys us some time," Dragos muttered, looking around the empty office.

Hashti stepped up on the Warden's desk, and punched the observation window free of the frame, sending it crashing to the ground below. Hashti laughed, waving to Pearl to come closer.

"Why? Just, why?" Simon asked, looking at the mess down below.

Hashti flashed a wide smile. "We are in a hurry, right?"

Simon rolled his eyes as the heavy equipment arm on Pearl's transport plucked him from the opening, bringing him inside. Hashti and Dragos jumped the gap, compartment hatch closing quickly behind them. Once everyone was safely aboard, Pearl turned to take them out of K Block. There was no resistance as she wove back through the automated material delivery lanes, and back out the front of the Teal District.

Back in the air over Orange Territory, Marjorie continued to rock back and forth, quietly listening to the electronic transmissions of the colony. Simon and Pearl did their best to try to listen in, her humming, beside the metallic drone of C.O.N. Dragos reloaded magazines while Hashti made tea in the small galley between the cockpit, and the crew quarters.

"The missing convicts, some of them, are from Earth. Recent arrivals, some former military, with power armor training," Simon said, watching the prison record capture scroll past on the HUD in his armor.

"What could Cerise do with that kind of personnel?" Hashti asked, handing Pearl a cup of tea. She sat in the cockpit beside her.

Simon thought about it for a moment, checking the listing for departure of any transports capable of deploying power armor. The display lit up with a handful of possibilities, but one seemed to interest Simon more than the others. Routing the information to Pearl's flight computer, she nodded and changed direction for the port.

"Union maintenance crew, heading out to work on the dome," Simon said, clapping his hand on the wall.

"That is odd?" Dragos asked.

"They're going out two shifts ahead of schedule. Union guys never show up to anything early. On time, maybe. Early, never," Pearl said, laughing.

"Only one of us is equipped for EVA," Hashti said, looking at Simon.

"I have Marshal Rider's Aegis on board, but it's set up for someone about the same size as the Marshal," Simon replied, looking at Pearl.

Pearl swung around, pointing at herself. "Ah! I get to be a deputy?"

Simon nodded.

"I can fly," Dragos said, nodding.

"Badly," Hashti said, eliciting a worried look from Pearl.

"It's true, but we'll be outside. Not much to run into, I hope," Dragos said.

"I can run the suit and my transport from my flight computer here," Pearl said, with a wink.

Simon held up his hands. "Whoa, we don't even know what they're doing. Let's pull their manifest and see if they are transmitting, like they're supposed to."

Marjorie nodded. "He's right. We don't know what they're doing."

Marjorie walked back to where Marshal Rider's Armor hung inside a compartment. She put her hand on the outside, armor inside lighting up at her approach. Marjorie smiled, turning to look at everyone else, who was looking at her.

"What?" Marjorie asked.

"You're some kind of telemechanic," Simon said. "Curious what you could do in a suit of armor like that."

"So are you," Marjorie replied, squinting.

Simon took a deep breath. "If you are talking to C.O.N., a little guidance would be appreciated."

Marjorie smiled a wry smile. "They shouldn't have tried to kill you guys and hurt the Marshal. My dad doesn't get attached to humans much anymore. He still has an affinity for people, because he remembers what it was like to be alone. To be the only."

"What does that mean?" Hashti asked.

Marjorie looked out a port window. "Mars is one of the few places where artificial intelligences have been killed. Targeted and killed by humans. It would have happened on the Lunar Colony as well, I'm told. Selene lost someone close to her, but managed to survive. It was a portent of what was coming."

Dragos nodded. "The fear of the machine."

"And, of Metasapients?" Hashti posited.

"My father, C.O.N., is not going to let the human's own nature destroy Mars, or any more of us. Too many good and noble humans sacrificed themselves for the rest to survive. My father wants to protect their legacy, and protect the protectors that remain," Marjorie said, her voice soft, easy on the ears.

"That sounds nice," Pearl said, Mars Port District lights appearing in the distance through the windshield in front of her.

Marjorie laughed. "The Cabal deployed a sonic weapon on Earth in Mexico, and did the same here. We couldn't do anything about what happened on Earth, but after gaining access to the autonomous system in the Teal District, we can do something about it here."

"You're saying we shouldn't look for Cerise, we should look for the weapon?" Simon asked, a little afraid of what an Omega Class AI like C.O.N., or Marjorie for that matter, could do with a high grade sonic weapon.

Marjorie blinked. "I hadn't thought about that, but yeah, maybe."

Simon frowned. "Do we chase Cerise outside the dome, or look for the weapon inside of it?"

Hashti looked sideways at Dragos. "Maybe we should do both?"

Dragos nodded. "Both is good."

Pearl set down at the Port of Mars, outfitting Dragos and Hashti with comms, and arranging transport for them with trusted members of the Teamsters Union. Marjorie stayed aboard with Pearl and Simon as they headed outside the Colony enclosure. The quick repairs to Pearl's transport held, as she performed a systems check in the port facility dry dock.

"We good," Pearl reported, pulling the transport around, and heading for the airlock that would take them outside.

Simon suited up, and locked into the first equipment crane harness. He checked the progression of the maintenance crew working outside the dome. So far, they had not deviated from their registered flight telemetry. He looked down the point list, along their route, trying to figure out what Cerise was up to, assuming she'd commandeered the maintenance crew's transport.

"The Communication Array is inside the last half of their planned route," Simon said, watching points on a map spread across the HUD in his Aegis Armor.

"She wants to make a call?" Pearl asked, a little dizzy from flying outside, with nothing to dodge or navigate around.

"Housed in the array, inside a shielded bulwark, is a quantum communications relay," Simon reported, bringing up a facility components list for the Mars Colony Communications Array.

Marjorie walked over in front of where Simon was suspended from the equipment crane harness. The compartment housing Marshal Rider's Aegis armor opened, the armor doing the same, allowing Marjorie to step inside it. Simon watched the HUD inside the Marshal's advanced Aegis suit boot up, Marjorie's face reflected just beyond the armored cowl.

"Going outside?" Simon asked, nervously.

Marjorie closed her eyes, voice sounding sleepy. "Only if I have to. Why would she want access to the array, Simon?"

"In theory, she could use it to send signals directly to C.O.N., bypassing the deep encryption that protects the Mars Colony, and facility maintenance programs within," Simon said, after thinking about it for a moment.

"She wants to try to 'hack' my father?"

"I don't know computers real well, but that seems like it would be hard," Pearl whispered over the comms, squinting at the horizon of the dome that sequestered the colony from the rest of Mars.

"Hack is probably the wrong word. She might be wanting to send a competing signal, change something about how the colony works at a facility administration level," Simon said, looking at a list of programming protocols that were set up to listen to the colony communications array.

"Any ideas?" Marjorie asked, sleepily, soft music playing over the comms as she spoke.

Simon shook his head. "There are literally hundreds of thousands of possible programming protocols she might be trying to influence. This, assuming we've guessed correctly what she intends to do."

Dragos came on over the comms, the sound of metal falling against concrete, playing out in the background. "Teamsters drop us off. We are at a compound in White District. No one is here, so far, but place is locked up tight."

"You need equipment to get in?" Simon asked.

The sound of more metal falling, and tempered glass breaking in the background was interrupted by Dragos laughing. "No, I have a Hashti. She is angry with this place."

Simon smiled. "Copy that."

Pearl's transport crested the rise, the colony communication array coming into view. A single facility maintenance transport could be seen beneath. A single suit of orange power armor was plodding along toward the communications array access point. Simon pulled up the hailing channel, and took a deep breath.

"This is Deputy Marshal Simon Vedter. Please transmit your operations certificate, and identify all personnel on board."

Cerise came back over the channel, her voice calm. "Hello, Simon."

Simon's face hardened. "Call your man back, or I'll go out and get him."

"You're a mechanic, not a police officer. You fix things, Simon. That's all I'm trying to do out here."

Simon squinted at the video capture of the facility maintenance transport. "You telling me you're actually out here on that facility maintenance transport, directing your minions, in person?"

"I'm out here with you, but I didn't commandeer just one transport, Simon."

ARTHUR WALKER

CHAPTER 18

TAJIKISTAN – SOUTHERN MOUNTAIN REGION – GROW FARM
0134

SEPTEMBER 14TH, 2201 – 11:37 PM

The transport was early, but Gulbadan expected this would be the case, after the last transport never arrived. She directed the Acrididae Metasapients to begin preparing the harvest for transport, guards tapping shock batons to remind them what would happen if they didn't move fast enough. The transport was older, sporting more International tags than was usual.

"Have you seen this one before?" Gulbadan asked one of the guards, gesturing toward the transport.

"I'm sure we have," he replied, eyes on the Acrididae as they carried burlap sacks from a truck to the loading platform.

Gulbadan pushed her balaclava up off of her face, and put her hand on her rifle. She pressed her finger to the comm in her ear, listening to the hailing channel for clearance.

"Hello," a deep voice said, in English, with a distinctly American accent.

"We will kill you if you come out armed, and shoot you down if you try to leave without identifying yourself properly," Gulbadan said, in her own impeccable English.

"If I come out, and any of you have weapons raised, I'll kill you. I'm not here for your product, I just want your workers."

Gulbadan motioned to her cohorts to get ready, waving one over carrying a rocket-propelled grenade. The crew access to the cockpit of the transport opened, a young man in a scarf, wearing a hoodie, and European jeans dropped to the ground. Dust popped off his well-worn boots, the holster on his belt, empty.

"Hi, my name is Royo," the young man said, holding up his hands. "I'd like to make a deal."

Gulbadan nodded, her dark eyes watching the transport carefully. "I am listening."

"My friend on the comms, and myself, have already liberated half of this Acrididae tribe in Mexico," Royo explained.

Several burlap sacks dropped to the ground, a couple dozen Acrididae Metasapients stopping to look up at Royo and sniffing the air. They turned their gaze angrily at their captors. Gulbadan noted the unease among her own men, outnumbered five to one by the workers. The Acrididae had a very distinct click that signaled when they were annoyed. Gulbadan had never heard the angry click, until now.

Gulbadan swallowed. "Go on."

Royo smiled. "The friend who I brought with my transport would prefer this was a bloodless exchange."

"So, he's inside?" Gulbadan said, eyes darting to her man with an RPG.

"Oh, I didn't say that," Royo said, looking around at the darkened hilltops nearby.

Gulbadan felt the hair on the back of her neck go up. She'd met the sort of people who flew these older transports. She knew how they kept their families, and that their friends were as much family as blood. They didn't bluff, and they did not play games.

Gulbadan lowered her rifle, raising a hand for the rest of her men to do the same. She could hear wind blowing over the hailing channel on the comm in her ear. Whomever was on the other side, had an elevated perch somewhere nearby. Listening intently, she could hear the rubber padding on a rifle stock compress.

"Put down the RPG, and every single rifle, and none of you has to die," the deep American voice said, the clack of pointed teeth as punctuation.

Gulbadan put her rifle down, but her man with the RPG brought his weapon up instead, blind devotion to the Cartel ruining his reason. He seemed to vanish, the round from a high powered rifle impacting the middle of the top of his head. Blood spattered across the interior of the loading platform, but little trace of him remained. The other Cartel soldiers quickly dropped their weapons and put their hands up.

"The Cartel will kill you for this," Gulbadan said, calmly. "This is not a threat, but a warning."

"The girl with a hammer sent me," the deep American voice replied, sending a chill through Gulbadan, and her associates. "Just be glad she did not come. She isn't as reasonable as I am."

Royo smiled, like it was any other polite transaction, opening the hatch to the cargo hold of his transport. The Acrididae Metasapients stepped forward sniffing Royo, and the transport. They seemed to titter and click with excitement, shuffling inside.

"Friend?" one of them said, putting a chitin-clad hand on Royo's chest.

"Heh, yep," Royo said, waving her inside.

Gulbadan, hands still raised, looked to Royo. "This girl with a hammer, she is real?"

Royo nodded, smile vanishing. "Yes."

"She just fights the Cartel?"

Royo shook his head. "She fights for the world. She fights for her friends," Royo said, gesturing to the Acrididae Metasapients crowding inside his cargo hold.

Gulbadan nodded. "I want to meet her."

A shadow fell across Gulbadan. A huge Ursine Metasapient, clad in armor, and carrying a highly customized rifle, climbed up on the loading dock. She turned, the color leaving her as she scrambled back. Her men fled, dropping their weapons and running hard into the night.

"What do you think, Royo?" Eamon said, a bead of sweat dropping from the tip of his nose.

Royo shrugged. "I have a couple of questions first."

Gulbadan scrambled to her feet, doing her best to compose herself.

"How long have you been under?" Royo asked, looking at Gulbadan, then up at Eamon.

Gulbadan looked shocked. "Um, since before the Shut Down. I was CGG International Police. I infiltrated the Cartel about four years ago. How did you know?"

"Didn't, for sure," Royo said. "Everyone ran from Eamon's badge, except you."

Gulbadan chuckled. "I didn't see his badge, but everyone in law enforcement has heard about the American Bear."

"There is no CGG, anymore. You stayed in the Cartel. Why should we trust you?" Eamon asked, eyes quietly scanning the dark around the landing platform.

Gulbadan gestured toward the wilderness around them. "I didn't have anywhere to go, and my handler inside the CGG Police kept taking my reports."

"Did you keep copies?" Eamon asked.

She hesitated, knowing she wasn't supposed to, for the purposes of operational integrity. "After the Shut Down, I started keeping copies."

Eamon nodded. "Good, that'll be your proof. Do we have all the Metasapients on site here?"

"Yes, and the copy of my records are encrypted on my comm."

Royo sighed. "I guess you better come with us, then."

"No," Gulbadan replied, taking the comm out of her ear and handing it to Eamon.

"Job isn't done," Eamon said, understanding her predicament. "Other people are counting on you."

"We are trying to find the head of the Cartel, and I think I'm close to him, or her."

Royo frowned. "There's no CGG, anymore. No job."

Eamon looked at Royo. "Just because there's no politicians, no bureaucrats, doesn't mean we stop being the police."

Gulbadan nodded. "That's right."

Royo held up his hands and went inside to start the pre-flight check.

"That said, the boy's not wrong. You don't have to do this," Eamon said, taking a copy of the data on Gulbadan's comm, and handing it back to her.

Gulbadan looked at Eamon's badge, bolted to his armor. "Yes, I do."

"Let me know when you're done, we will come get you."

"I'll make my own way."

Eamon nodded. "Figured you might, but it felt impolite not to offer."

"It's good to know some of us are still out there, working."

Eamon nodded. "Likewise, officer."

"What I said before, about wanting a meet with the girl with a hammer…" Gulbadan said, looking around.

Eamon turned to go, giving a wave over his shoulder. "I'll let her know."

Royo took his freight hauler up slowly, making sure he stayed well below conventional radar detection. From the cargo hold, the familiar sound of happy Acrididae Metasapients clicking to one another filled his ears. Eamon curled up in the galley, taking up the entire compartment, rifle hung from a pot hook by the tiny stove. Royo headed west, gaining altitude only after they crossed the Red Sea, crossing into Egyptian airspace.

Royo hit the comm and broadcasted a spoofed transponder signal identifying himself as a Sudanese Relief Transport operating with Uroboros Financial credentials. What Egyptian Governmental authority there was, cleared him for flight. He gained altitude as he gained speed, Acrididae Metasapients preparing the dehydrated food that Eamon gathered earlier.

Eamon's mobile lit up, buzzing quietly in the clip attached to the front of his duty vest. He tapped it with his paw, grumbling as he shut his eyes again. Brook's face appeared on the display, camera looking out toward the cockpit, Royo glancing back over his shoulder.

"Royo, is Eamon there?" Brook asked.

Royo looked at the sleeping bear, and shook his head. "Nope."

"The intelligence gathered at the grow farm checks out. We've managed to make contact with an entire wing of the CGG Police that has been operating on shadow funds skimmed from illicit Cartel operations. They wouldn't give me details, but they sound close to pulling the Cartel down in most of Asia," Brook said, silvery eyes reflecting the backlighting on her own mobile, background behind her dark.

Royo smiled. "Cool."

"You have the rest of the Acrididae Metasapients?"

Royo nodded. "Yep, I'll have them in the drop zone in Ukkusiksalik by morning."

"Try to convince Eamon to go with them." Brook asked, gently. "For me."

Eamon opened one eye, looking at Royo. Royo shrugged. "I'll do my best."

Taylor crouched down into the view, face hugging up beside Brook's. Royo did his best to look like he was flying casual, but Taylor's quiet laughter quickly burned through his façade. Tears in Royo's eyes, he nodded to Taylor.

"It's gonna be alright," Taylor said, her blue green hair glowing in the dark of wherever she and Brook were calling from.

"I know, but I spent a lot of time thinking it wouldn't be," Royo said, smiling weakly.

"I forget, all the time, that you are as much Vance Uroboros, as Kale is. Or, Silverstein, for that matter. If there is anything to forgive, I forgive it. If there was ever any pain, I don't feel it anymore. All is well," Taylor said, watching Royo wipe his eyes with a sleeve.

"Okay," Royo replied, voice shaking.

"When you're done, come home," Taylor said, smiling warmly.

Royo sniffed, composing himself. "I will."

Brook reached out, pressing a button off screen, ending the call. Eamon opened both eyes, and looked at Royo, even though his gaze was fixed firmly out the windshield toward the horizon. Eamon had seen every version of Vance Uroboros still walking the planet, every person that shared that extended identity. They each bore the weight of it differently, but Royo seemed to take the responsibility for mending the world more personally.

"You tell me to get off in Canada, I will," Eamon said, patting Royo on the shoulder.

Royo smirked, cocky attitude reasserting itself. "You ever need a ride, I will come get you."

CHAPTER 19

SOMEWHERE IN SANTIAGO FLORES, SAN LUIS POTOSI, MEXICO – THE FACTORY

SEPTEMBER 12TH, 2201 – 2:59 PM

Doctor Helmet looked across the floor at his two colleagues, each having already expired from their wounds. The high ceiling overhead, fluorescent lights shining down on the laboratory workshop, danced with Vivian's sinister shadow as she ransacked filing cabinets, and shook notebooks, looking for something. Doctor Helmet winced, trying to sit up, but he couldn't feel most of the right side of his body.

"Maybe if you told me what you were looking for, I could help you?" Doctor Helmet asked, prompting a metallic growl of frustration from Vivian.

She loomed over Doctor Helmet, his wounded state reflecting back at him from the visor covering her face. Her berserker class cyborg body was awash in blood and the stink of burnt flesh, the end of the plasma thrower mounted on her shoulder, still aglow. Doctor Helmet wiped blood from his mouth with the sleeve on his left arm.

"I hate you. I've always hated you," Vivian sneered, taking a small measure of delight in Doctor Helmet's suffering.

"You blame me for what happened to him," Doctor Helmet said, matter of fact.

"You and every replica you made of your wretched self," Vivian whispered as she knelt down beside him.

"Would you, truly, rather be dead, and Doctor Madmar still alive?"

Vivian nodded.

Doctor Helmet smiled. "He didn't deserve you."

Vivian kicked Doctor Helmet across the laboratory, through an observation window, and into a monitoring chamber. He coughed up teeth, and chunks of esophagus as he breathed what would be one of a few of his last breaths. Vivian gingerly opened the side door to the monitoring chamber and sat down, resting an elbow on the recording station where Doctor Helmet lay.

"Acero never turned up, did he? The Cartel will be coming, and pretty soon," Doctor Helmet whispered.

Vivian nodded. "I know. It'll take them a little time to gather up the enhanced soldiers they'll need. I do have a little time left."

"Plan to spend all of it kicking me around?" Doctor Helmet asked, genuinely curious.

Vivian reached over, powerful cyborg claw grasping Doctor Helmet by the neck. She jerked his head to one side, producing an audible snap before letting him go.

"You've got a point, for once," Vivian said, using her comm implant to access the private facility grid.

She searched for her sisters, Tellus Mater, and The Factory, but they were both offline. It was too soon for the Cartel to have arrived, and the Mexican Military would still be sifting through the aftermath in Mexico City. Vivian frowned, switching to broadcast over the public announcement channel.

"Ezra One," she said, voice polluted with a strange lilt in the digitizing element.

Deep in the bowels of the Factory, Ezra One looked up, hearing Vivian speak his name over the PA. He squinted back into the darkness toward the point of egress, the watery route that would take him out again. The same way he'd gone decades previous. Hefting the satchel containing the inactive sentience cores of The Factory, and Tellus Mater, Ezra wished there was some other way to handle Vivian.

He hated that The Factory might have been right.

He could just leave and let the Cartel deal with her. There were still children inside, and while he knew Gelt wouldn't hurt them, Ezra didn't want him to have them. Going back in, and facing Vivian, was the only way.

Vivian reached the sentience core chamber, finding the blast doors undamaged, but open. She stepped inside, and looked up. At the center of the silicone and copper eye that made up the chamber, there was a gaping hole where The Factory's sentience core once controlled the facility. Back-ups hummed along the walls, keeping essential functions going, but the room was otherwise silent and untouched.

Vivian flew through the personnel tunnels toward the descent into the lower levels, anti-gravitic hooks silently pulling her metallic form through the air. Her enhanced sensors couldn't detect even a chemical signature in the air, or any other indication that anyone had passed by the threshold but her. She knew some of the Drones could be stealthy, but Ezra One seemed to have abilities far beyond the scope of those recorded by The Factory.

Thinking better of trying to chase a Type One Drone in the darkness below, she turned to head back. Ezra One stepped out into her path, about ten meters ahead. It was as though the shadows gave birth, and Ezra was their child. Even standing in visual range, her other sensors were telling her that nothing was there.

"I can get the kids out of here, without your help," Ezra One said, his silhouette dancing like the shadow of a candle across the HUD of Vivian's cybernetic visual sensors.

Vivian blinked her biological eyes, even though her enhanced visual aids never did so.

"But, it'd be better for everyone if you stepped out of that battle frame, and just came with me."

"I can't," Vivian said, clawed vambraces shaking.

"Why not?" Ezra One asked, his inky outline wavering at the edges.

Vivian used her own telemechanical prowess to reach out. The corridor was flooded with nanotechnological particles, each with their own synthetic telemechanical and electromagnetic signature. Vivian opened the cowl on her armor, visor sliding back, to get a look with her own eyes, trying to pick Ezra One out of the static.

As the cowl clicked into place, Ezra One's left fist connected with Vivian's brow, just above her nose. She staggered back, spark and smoke dancing across her vision as drug delivery countermeasures hissed, pushing adrenaline to keep her awake. She sank to her knees, power quickly fading from the battle frame connected to her cyborg likeness. Ezra One stood three feet away, his right hand grasping a handful of components from her cyborg armor, necessary for power delivery.

Vivian laughed. "Never had a chance, did I?"

"Offer still stands," Ezra One said, tossing the components aside, and adjusting the satchel over his shoulder.

"It's not much of a choice, at this point," Vivian said, voice digitizer losing power, audio output clicking over to her own damaged vocal cords.

"Tellus Mater told me that you had a plan to get the kids out if your attempt to get the qCPU failed. It has failed, Vivian. Tell me how to get the kids out of here, and before Gelt and his friends arrive."

Vivian punched out of her battle frame, staggering out of it with her replacement cyborg body. It was lovely, obviously made by hand for her, by someone that loved her. It had all the styling of something Doctor Maurice Madmar would have crafted, before he was driven insane.

"It's nice," Ezra One said, taking note of how realistic and soft it looked, while retaining the obvious craftsmanship of an artist.

Vivian hugged herself, and closed her eyes. "It's all I have left of Maurice, in so many ways."

Ezra One grabbed Vivian and pulled her out of the way as her cyborg armor rose up on its own, hollow digitized voice issuing forth a strange metallic cackle. Pushing Vivian behind cover, the armor engaged hidden emergency power, and brought the plasma thrower to bear, firing a salvo. Ezra was able to get clear, the extreme heat burning off the nanotechnological particles floating in the corridor.

Ezra leapt from a crouched position on the wall, dragging his claws across the underside of the cyborg armor. Stabilizing agent, and hyper-refined hydraulic fluid spilled out as the armor clattered to the ground, plasma thrower malfunctioning and melting through the floor. The blackened stealth components across the outside of the armor broke apart like cheap pottery revealing the blood red alloy armor beneath.

The audio digitizer onboard continued to cackle ominously until Ezra One ripped the cowl off, and kicked the armor down the descent to the lower levels of the factory. A dull roar flew past as the armor exploded somewhere down below in the middle of falling.

"Kaspersky," Ezra One hissed, dropping the cowl of the cyborg armor down the shaft as well.

"He killed them. He almost killed me," Vivian said, kneeling beside the satchel that had been carrying the sentience cores of The Factor and Tellus Mater.

The plasma salvo had incinerated both cores, burning Ezra's satchel to cinders, all but a short length of the strap. Vivian covered her face, the one biological tear duct she had left, intermittently wetting her eye and cheek as she mourned her lost sisters. Ezra came up beside her, and looked down at the remnants, feeling his own strange well of emotion for his lost step mother.

"Vivian, the Cartel is still coming. There are still kids up above."

Vivian stood, the sinister quality that seemed to hold her in thrall before, was utterly gone. "I know, we can mourn later. Let's get them, and ourselves, out of here."

As they walked through the laboratory workshop area, Vivian paused, looking down at what remained of the three Doctors Helmet. Ezra One wasn't shocked by the scene, having seen the bloody state of Vivian's cyborg armor. Still, Vivian staggered, almost as if wounded, through the room.

"Everything I did while I was wearing the armor felt like a dream. I didn't want to believe that I'd done all these things," Vivian whispered, tapping in a code at a locked door.

Ezra One watched the door slide to one side. Eight children sat in a bunker-like dwelling beyond. They each hesitated until Vivian called to them. It was though none of them had ever seen her without the armor, or heard her speak without the Mother's Voice of The Factory. Ezra One empathized with the kids, knowing something of what they were feeling.

It would be hard for them to learn to trust again.

They went to an ancient hangar, a single operational transport within. It was squared off at the front under the cargo netting that covered it. Vivian struggled to pull the netting down, revealing an old freight hauler, a decade or two older than even what Tullia and Royo flew. It was marked with CGG teal, white stripes, and lettering.

"Haven't seen the old CGG pattern on anything in thirty years," Ezra One said, putting a clawed hand on the side.

"It was mine, back when I flew for ..." Vivian stopped mid-sentence, looking up at the red lights flashing along the wall where it met with the ceiling.

"Cartel?" Ezra One asked, trying to get the hangar door controls to respond.

"Someone just breached the lower levels, and is making their way through to the facility layer," Vivian explained, hastily powering up the freight hauler and skipping past all the pre-flight checks.

"Your old freight hauler outrun a Cartel transport?" Ezra One asked, watching the children climb aboard.

Vivian shook her head, a look of fear crossing her face.

"Then I guess I better give them something else to do," Ezra One said, clawing the housing off the hangar door controls, stripping two wires and touching them together.

The hangar doors sprang to life, slowly rising. Vivian watched Ezra One drop out of sight, to the exterior of the facility as she slowly flew out, keeping her engines low, and running lights off. Down below, a single sleek transport sat beside the drainage port access to the factory. The dull glow of a cigarette lit up the Cartel soldier's face as he looked up, spotting Vivian's freight hauler.

It was the last thing he would ever do, as Ezra One made contact with him. Vivian couldn't see what happened between the distance, and the darkness, but there was a loud pop inside the transport below. She lingered there for a moment, before turning to head down and get a closer look. Twenty feet from the ground, she couldn't see anything, except smoke rising from the inside of the transport.

Ezra One slammed into the side of the freight hauler, fist banging on the crew access door. Startled, Vivian opened it for him, allowing him to scramble in. Ezra One looked angrily at her, hand sleek with blood.

"That was dumb, you should have just flown away."

Vivian looked sadly at the controls, pushing the throttle as they gained altitude. "You didn't leave me behind."

Ezra One softened. "I almost did. I came back for the kids, pretty sure I'd have to kill you."

Vivian sulked.

"Knowing what I know now, about that cyborg armor of yours, I'm glad things turned out how they did," Ezra One said in a low voice, looking back to make sure the children were alright.

Vivian reached for the comm, but Ezra One stopped her, placing his hand over hers. "No, we don't call out until we're over Mexico City. It isn't safe. Just keep flying to Mexico City, alright?"

Vivian nodded, feeling numb, and bewildered.

Vivian flew for three hours, exhausted by the time they reached Mexico City. Ezra One pointed her toward a plain looking warehouse, with high concrete walls. Ezra instructed her to bring the freight hauler beside the second story wall, and wait. As she did, the wall parted, revealing a secret hangar. Inside, she could see Brook, Taylor AI, and Heavy Dub waiting on the platform, beside a table with water, and sack lunches.

Vivian brought the transport in slowly, old landing gear creaking loudly as they touched down inside the warehouse hangar. As soon as they were clear, the hangar doors snapped shut. The children murmured fearfully as the transport powered down, looking around as the interior grew dark.

"It'll be okay," Vivian said, doing her best to reassure them as she worked through the post flight checklist, and opened the cargo hold doors. Light flooded into the interior as the children stepped out onto the platform. The smell of hastily prepared food made Ezra One's stomach growl. It had been a while since he'd had a proper meal.

Taylor ran to Ezra One as he stepped out of the transport and into the warehouse hangar. She wrapped her arms around him. "I thought I lost you in there," Taylor whispered, hugging Ezra tightly.

"Almost did. We did lose everyone, except the kids," Ezra reported, hugging her back.

"And, Vivian," Taylor said, looking over at Vivian beside the children from the transport to the table of supplies..

Ezra looked over at Brook. "Yeah, about that…"

Brook's ears twitched at the mention of her name, but she continued to stand beside Heavy Dub, while the kids got something to eat. Heavy Dub looked to Ezra One, pointed at Vivian, and mouthed the words, "what the fuck?"

Ezra One looked into Heavy Dub's eyes, drew a line on his own neck where Heavy Dub had a wide scar. Heavy Dub had gotten that scar after his own cybernetics had been hacked. He nodded to Ezra, lowering his head slightly, memories of difficult times flooding back into his mind.

After the children were put into temporary quarters, Brook met with Ezra One, Taylor, Heavy Dub, and the Cyberdoc, to check Vivian over. The Cyberdoc checked her cybernetic systems, gave her a green light, minus some exhaustion to her original biological semblance. As he left, Vivian stared at the floor, her quiet telemechanical aura turned inward.

"Ezra, what aren't you telling me?" Brook asked.

"Under the stealth treatment of Vivian's cyborg armor, there was a familiar red hue. After she detached from it, the frame sprang to life, killing The Factory and Tellus Mater. It laughed at me the entire time, like it was possessed by a ghost," Ezra One explained, putting a hand on Brook's arm.

Brook nodded. "Kaspersky."

Vivian looked up. "Kaspersky? The Man in Red? The one who…"

The room fell silent for a moment. Taylor reached out her hand to Vivian. "Hold my hand."

Vivian complied, lowering her own telemechanical defenses so that it would be easier for Taylor to read her. Taylor's hair went from blue green, to blinding white. Taylor's eyes darted back and forth, as if she was looking at billions of lines of code at once, dancing in space around her. Vivian looked uncomfortable for a moment, but soon relaxed as indicator lights across, and internal to, her own cyborg body turned from a reddish pink, to a silvery white.

"What did you do?" Vivian asked, breathing a little easier.

Taylor shrugged, looking at her own hand. "I'm not really sure. I was just trying to get a sense of you, see what my own latent abilities could tell me."

Vivian looked at her hand, the remnants of what looked like metallic glitter sticking to her palm. "I remember everything I did now, but it feels like there's a piece of glass between me and all of that. It wasn't my fault, and I wasn't in control."

"From records we've captured from different Cabal facilities, we think a dozen suits of that cyborg armor were made. We've found and destroyed nine of them. Wearing the armor is really bad for you, whether you're a cyborg, or a nanotechnological contrived being," Brook explained, the memory of what it did to Kale still fresh in her mind.

Vivian nodded, looking sullenly at the floor. "Where is Vance Uroboros?"

Heavy Dub picked up a call on his mobile, and stepped out of the room, giving Brook a knowing expression. She nodded, her slate gray skin creasing slightly around the eyes. Vivian looked from Brook, to Ezra One, to Taylor, each seemed to be holding their breath.

Heavy Dub leaned back in, putting his mobile away, and giving Brook the thumbs up.

"Right now, he's in three different places at once, trying to bring Earth, Mars, and the Lunar Colony back together," Brook said, breathing a sigh of relief.

Vivian looked up. "How can I help?"

"There is something you can do," Brook replied, motioning for Vivian to follow her.

They walked back through the Uroboros Financial Safe Site to a small warehouse. In it were several cargo containers. Brook picked up the call controls, and had the crane bring down an orange container, locked with a simple padlock. The automated crane set the container down on the warehouse floor.

Brook grabbed the padlock, breaking it with a quick tug, startling Vivian. "I forgot how strong you are."

"It's everything we were able to collect from Earth and the Lunar Colony," Brook said, opening the container.

Inside were all of Doctor Maurice Madmar's personal possessions, his journals, vinyl record collection, college yearbooks, and research notes. Everything had a cataloging tag attached, as Uroboros Financial investigators had gone over every single thing inside, but it was everything. Everything that Vivian could remember, anyway.

Vivian nodded, smiling through tears. "What do you need me to do?"

"Nothing, really. We weren't sure what to do with his things. Maybe you have an idea or two?" Brook said, waving as if to give Vivian permission to go into the container.

"Maurice told me what he wanted to do with his life. Many times." Vivian looked around the container, picking up a stack of old photographs.

"Take all the time you need. I have a few things to handle, but I'll have Heavy Dub come check on you in a bit."

Vivian smiled, pausing on a photo of her, standing with Doctors Madmar and Helmet, before the MDC Project. She could see in herself, and her friends, the desire to not just save the world, but make it better.

"Thank you, Brook."

CHAPTER 20

PORT DISTRICT, FAUSTIO'S CANTINA – LUNAR COLONY

SEPTEMBER 13TH, 2201 – 10:21 PM

It was a lot cleaner than he remembered, and a lot of the local personality had faded away. The smaller eating establishments near the port were all pretty much the same, but there were a lot more Metasapients in charge, instead of just serving. The public announcement boards were all electronic, advertising Martian Roller Derby, local artists, concerts, and things that had to do with the humanities.

Gone were the corporate sponsors, and endless advertising. Gelt looked up across the park, to a large central column for the Lunar Colony dome. Playing on a huge display, was an interview with Taylor IA, talking about next steps for rebuilding the colonies throughout the system and Earth. Gelt waited a little longer than he would have liked for an auto lift, but it came clean, the interior quiet, as opposed to a minute of music beside ten minutes of ads.

Fautios was, thankfully, unchanged. It was still dingy, pretending to be upscale, and obviously run by the local Syndicate. It did a little to set Gelt at ease, seeing the usual entertainment was still available, standard vices still up for sale. Some things never change, and Gelt was glad.

Once inside, he looked around for anyone he knew, but it had been a while. Resigned, he asked for his reservation, a server leading him to a private table. In a booth big enough to seat four people.

Gelt sat down in the booth, the other two gentlemen shifting over to make room. He waved for the server who brought him a menu. Gelt glanced over it, made his selection almost instantly. The server nodded, and headed off to fill his order.

Gioele Faustio looked over at his cousin, Pasquale, then to Gelt.

Gelt held his mobile in one hand, scrolling the contents of the screen with his thumb, eyes hidden by the brim of his hat. As his order arrived, Gelt put his mobile away, and looked up at Gioele. Pasquale sighed, leaning back in his seat.

"We all right, here?" Gelt asked, pushing his food around with a fork.

"I get the feeling this isn't a meet between us, and you," Gioele said, folding his hands, and placing them on the table.

Gelt nodded, taking his hat off and hanging it on the light fixture suspended over the table.

"We aren't getting a lot from the ground in Mexico, but what we are getting doesn't sound too good," Pasquale said.

"Lunar Syndicate had a similar issue, from what I understand," Gelt said, taking a bite.

Gioele sighed. "Yeah, well, the new administration lets us live legitimately, with only a little oversight on the gambling side. What you're asking us to do, goes outside the boundaries of legitimate."

Gelt looked up from his plate. "Are you backing out?"

Pasquale looked sideways at his cousin. "We haven't made up our minds."

"You have a counteroffer?" Gelt asked, dabbing his lips with a cloth napkin.

"Local administration wants to meet with a Cartel representative. We told them the answer would probably be no, given the political climate up here, but that we'd ask."

Gioele nodded to his cousin. "So, we're asking."

"This negotiation lets you stay legitimate, but with a little room to maneuver," Gelt muttered, shaking his head.

"Yeah, well, you know how it is. When politicos can't make a thing happen all legal up in lights, they keep a handful of us around for things like this. You have someone with you that could take that meeting?" Gioele asked, hopeful.

"I'll handle it myself," Gelt replied, surprising both of the Faustios.

"Oh, wow, that'd be great. Well, then, consider the other thing handled," Pasquale said, shaking Gelt's hand.

"Oh, also, your usual accommodations, and entertainment, is set aside for you. For as long as you want to stay," Gioele said, standing up and shaking Gelt's hand.

"You had that good of a time when you visited Mexico last time?" Gelt said, taking his hat off the light, and putting it back on his head.

"Oh, hell yeah," Gioele replied. "Cartel crew really knows how to throw a party."

Gelt watched them go, certain he'd been betrayed, favor with the Lunar Criminal Syndicate already hanging by a thread before things fell through in Mexico. The server brought him a slip of paper, in the guise of a bill, but all that was written on it was an address and a time. Gelt had about ninety minutes before the meet, not long enough to arrange getting back off the Lunar Colony, and without the Faustios being aware.

"I guess I play this out," Gelt muttered, leaning back, and tipping his hat down low.

Gelt took his time finishing his meal, and drinking Faustio's best liquor, before heading out to catch an automated lift. It would only take him within walking distance of the location, a place where colony surveillance would be minimal, and foot traffic non-existent. He took the time to walk the distance, surprised to see vagrants, and an actual homeless population foraging through the trash bins.

"New administration smells a lot like the old administration," Gelt thought quietly to himself, walking quietly past, and keeping to the shadows. The lights of the lunar colony didn't reach this area, out past the trash pickup, near an old industrial park. He walked past an old motorcycle, left to rust by the side of the vehicle access road.

Ahead he could see someone standing next to a nice ground transport, wearing a suit and tie. The driver was attempting to shoo away a vagrant, picking up a pipe to threaten him. Condensation from the containment dome rained down in the area, fog rising from the water collection trenches below. Gelt wandered up, wondering if the meet was real.

"I'm here for the meet," Gelt said, keeping the brim of his hat low.

"Ah, good, finally. My name is Agapito. I'm Selene AI's attendant, and her eyes and ears on the street." Gelt nodded, the name and association checking out with what he remembered about the Lunar AI, and her new Terrestrial IA assistant.

"What can I do for you?"

"There is local opposition to my being the Steward for the Facility AI. They want a 'real' person."

"How do I fix that for you?"

"Every movement has a leader, and the local opposition to my being the steward is no different. We need someone, from the outside, to... influence her."

Gelt reached into his pocket, fished out a cigarette, and lit it. Agapito's driver turned quickly, using the distraction from the flame on the lighter, to hit Gelt across the head with a pipe. A bioelectric arc jumped from the driver's arm, striking Gelt as he went down.

Agapito reacted with genuine surprise, and shock. "What the hell, Kale?"

Kale took the chauffeur's hat off, and placed it on Agapito's head. "You did well. Very convincing."

"That's because you didn't tell me you were going to do that!" Agapito bellowed, pointing to Gelt laying on the ground, blood flowing freely from a gash across his forehead.

"He will be alright, Agapito. Trust me, I have done this before," Kale said, smiling faintly.

Kale cradled Gelt's head and waived smelling salts under his nose. Gelt sputtered, doing his best to open his eyes, but one was already swollen shut. He looked first up at Agapito, no recognition in his eye, then to Kale.

"What happened? Who are you guys?" Gelt said, wincing as he reached up and touched his head wound.

Kale looked down, with genuine concern, pulled his mobile out of his pocket, and held it up. "You called us, boss. Sounded like you were in some kind of trouble, so we came straight over."

Gelt nodded, slowly, doing his best to hide his confusion. "Right, of course. Get me out of here."

"Right away, boss. What were you even doing out here?" Kale said, helping Gelt up into the car.

"I was… handling some business, got jumped," Gelt stammered, looking around at the area, still trying to hide his bewilderment.

Agapito sat down in the driver's seat, moving the seat forward, and checking the mirrors. "Um, where to?"

Gelt blinked, trying to recall where he should ask to be taken, but nothing was coming to him. Kale let the uncomfortable silence linger for a moment, before barking orders at Agapito.

"Faustio's, and make it quick. Boss has a doctor there, and I'm starving," Kale said, clapping Agapito on the shoulder.

Agapito nodded, pulling the ground transport around. "You got it."

CHAPTER 21

SEPTEMBER 14TH, 2201 – 8:09 AM

Pearl lowered Simon down using the onboard equipment crane, magnetic boot clamps allowing him to walk along the metallic joiner down in the seam between two huge pieces of the biological enclosure. Ahead, he could see Moses Vale, lumbering along toward the array, his Mining Company power armor outfitted with a single powered implement, one designed to open airlock doors.

The Facility Maintenance Transport between Simon and Moses began offloading more individuals in orange power armor, but they clearly had weapons. As soon as Simon was boots down, Pearl flew ahead, turning at a sharp angle so that her equipment crane would snag that of the other transport. The individual in power armor making the descent to the enclosure below was instead flung like a rag doll.

They fell, at a sharp arc, but not shallow enough to avoid falling the full distance from the initial curve of the dome, to the Martian ground below. The Facility Maintenance Transport tried to break free, gunning their engines. As they did, Pearl jettisoned her own equipment crane. Throttling up for a hard pull, the other transport overshot, turning hard into the biological dome.

The damage wasn't total, but their cabin pressure was compromised, forcing them to head back to port. Pearl powered up her second equipment crane, and brought her transport around. Moses Vale had already entered the communications array, and Simon was lingering next to the open airlock.

"Pearl, you all right?" Simon asked, looking back.

"Lost e-crane one, but I've got two coming online. I can still extract you if you need," Pearl said, nudging the throttle so she was slowly coming up over Simon's position on the dome.

"Marshal Service Cadets are already moving to intercept the other transport at the port, I'm going after Moses Vale," Simon reported, his Aegis armor switching illuminators on as he went through the airlock.

"Be careful," Pearl said, looking back over her shoulder at Marjorie, eyes closed, inside Marshal Rider's Aegis suit.

Simon kept his pistol in its locked holster, knowing he'd have to go hands on with Moses inside the array. The interior was much as the schematics Simon had studied suggested. The facility was full of huge copper coils, miles of thick fiber optic cable, access panels to different components that had to be sequestered from one another, metal walkways leading up and down the interior of the building-sized housing, and darkness. Moses Vale had already vanished from sight, but Simon had a good idea where he was heading.

"Moses, the only way out of here is with me," Simon said, over the public frequency.

"You say that, but it tells me that you haven't guessed what Cerise's plan is," Moses replied, static coming back over with his voice.

"She told you?" Simon replied, incredulous.

"Oh, hell no, but I guessed it pretty quick," Moses replied, the sound of powered actuators running in the background.

"Radiation shielding around the quantum relay is pretty strong. Your suit isn't rated for it. You'll get cooked in there if C.O.N. decides to call out," Simon said, taking some metal stairs upward.

"That's a pretty good bluff, Deputy Marshal Vedter. Having been contracted to move a qCPU, I know all about their environmental tolerances, and such. Anyway, I wasn't headed that way," Moses replied, laughing.

Simon paused, mid-step, looking up, and then down again.

"Ooh, I bet, right now, you're wondering if I'm bluffing," Moses said, the sound of an airlock popping open in the background.

Simon broke into a run, heading up toward the quantum relay access, following the schematics on his HUD. As he rounded the last corner, he could see the access point fifty feet down a long, sensor-filled corridor. Simon paused, looking back over his shoulder, cursing under his breath.

"Outsmarted yourself, did you?" Moses said, static crackling over the connection.

Simon turned, and slowly headed back, frustration boiling over. "It doesn't matter, I'm going to bring you in."

"I'm counting on it my friend. I'm counting on it," Moses said, with a chuckle.

On the other side of the biological enclosure, on the opposite side the colony, near the original build site, Cerise waited outside a large set of blast doors. Above them, they were marked, "A Block - Cell Sector 00001 – Alpha District". The lettering after A Block had been added a while after the initial characters.

Cerise waited patiently, checking the time on her analogue wristwatch.

The indicator light over the blast doors lit up, doors shuddering as power hit the old hydraulic enclosures. They groaned loudly as they opened, old yellow paint flaking off, and falling to the floor with no small amount of dust. Cerise smiled. Moses had pulled it off.

The doors lost power and failed, having only opened about eighteen inches, but there was plenty of room for Cerise to slip through. She walked past an ancient processing office, where the very first convicts were brought to Mars, the shackles put on, never to come off again.

Picking up a chair, Cerise threw it through the one way mirror glass into observation, and climbed through into the first precinct of the Martian Law Enforcement Division, marked M-LED, with a six-pointed star next to it. Dust billowed up around her boots with each step she took, pushing past rotting wooden doors, past offices, and into the ancient mainframe chamber that was still running.

Beneath layers of dust, old LCD displays slowly scrolled ancient arrest and incarceration records. The central mainframe still had connectivity to the current system, but it was slow to upload the current record. Cerise smiled, looking at decades old arrest reports that were just appearing on the main system. She looked up at the old drop ceiling over the mainframe, amazed the place was still intact.

"I thought about doing this as well," Silverstein said, leaning up against the entrance, pushing the old wooden door aside.

Cerise nearly jumped out of her skin, whirling around, a shiv in hand.

"Ouroboru, you almost scared me to death," Cerise said, putting her hand on her chest to steady her heart.

Silverstein raised an eyebrow.

"Silverstein. Sorry, I know that's what you prefer now."

"Awfully polite toward someone you're probably planning to shiv."

Cerise laughed, throwing the shiv upward, sticking it in the ceiling.

Silverstein smirked. "You're really going to do it?"

"I read the Cabal report, when you were here, um … a while back. That thing, with the wardens. Did you know Ezra One was here when that all went down?" Cerise said, sitting cross-legged on yellowing papers, strewn across the floor.

Silverstein nodded, wishing he could smoke in the room without setting off all the dry paper and timbers.

"It's weird, seeing you here. The Dragon brought you?" Cerise said, leaning forward, putting her face in her hands.

"Yeah," Silverstein said, sliding down the door frame until he was sitting across from Cerise.

Cerise lowered her head. "Do you think if you'd come here, and done it back then, that the Shut Down would have worked as you wanted it to?"

Silverstein shrugged. "I don't know. I was scared, worried the rest of the Cabal would figure out what I was up to."

Cerise giggled, the hard prison exterior dropping away for a moment. "They were clueless. You were afraid for nothing."

"My friends were good at keeping my secrets."

Cerise lay back on the floor, gathering a stack of papers under head for a pillow. "I'm tired, Silverstein."

"I know."

"So what happens now? You take me back, and I float in a water bubble with the rest of the Cabal, in deep space forever?"

Silverstein shook his head. "Naw."

Cerise looked over at Silverstein, who was looking up at the shiv in the ceiling, an amused expression on his face. She stood up, walked over to the ancient mainframe, and pulled up a command prompt. Entering several commands she'd spent the last decade memorizing, she hit enter, and then would wait a moment before entering in more commands.

"Command Priority Alpha," Cerise whispered, turning to walk over and sit next to Silverstein.

"You remember to enter commands as an administrator?" Silverstein teased.

Cerise laughed, sitting down next to him.

"Does it hurt?" Cerise asked, after a couple minutes.

Silverstein shook his head. "Not that I recall."

"You've never used it on anyone?" Cerise asked, incredulous.

Silverstein shook his head. "No one I wasn't supposed to."

Cerise took a deep breath, and leaned against Silverstein. "I'm ready."

"Not here, too much history," Silverstein said, pushing himself up, and offering Cerise his hand.

Cerise looked at Silverstein, a look of confusion crossing her face. "What about Gelt?"

Silverstein shrugged, and motioned for her to follow him. They walked back through the ancient Martian facility, Silverstein taking his jacket off, and hanging it on a chair outside the blast door entrance to Block A. He slipped off his shoes, and socks, as well. Cerise looked on, concerned.

"It's all right. We won't need them where we're going."

Cerise shrugged, kicking off her boots, and her teal prison jumpsuit. They walked to where Shwalishi hovered, just off the dock from where Cerise's unlisted transport was parked. The ancient alien vessel chimed, opening her passenger compartment for Silverstein and Cerise. They climbed aboard, Shwalishi vanishing twenty minutes before Marshal Service cadets would respond, and find a baffling scene.

Silverstein and Cerise slept the journey away, Shwalishi slowing down near an island in the South Pacific. As they disembarked, warm water hit their feet, the setting sun dropping low in the distance. Silverstein turned, placing his hand on the alien vessel.

"Thank you, old friend. Goodbye," he whispered.

The Dragon chimed, becoming water, slipping away into the surf. Cerise looked around at the abandoned island, a handful of tourist spots still with power. She scanned the coastline, and the forest up above the rocks, seeing no sign of anyone. No footprints in the sand, no smoke in the air, no grind of engines in the distance.

"Are you going to just leave me here?" Cerise asked, crossing her arms in front of her chest.

Silverstein walked up beside her. "No, I'm going to stay here with you."

"I don't understand," Cerise said.

"Look at yourself," Silverstein said, nodding down at her.

Cerise looked down, expecting to see the endless roadmap of scars and prison tattoos, the evidence of having lost her ability to have children long ago. She expected to see the reminders of every bad thing that had happened in the last six thousand years since they met Golgotha. It was all gone, only her own unblemished skin remained.

Cerise looked up at Silverstein, noticing the scar over his eye, the one given to him by Kale, was also gone. She sat down in the surf, overwhelmed, and not sure what to say. Silverstein pulled out his mobile, turning it around to show the screen was dark, and that it was powered off.

"I can, really easily, turn this on. Or, I can throw it as hard as I can out into the surf. What do you say?"

Cerise reached up, took Silverstein's mobile, and threw it as far as she could. It splashed somewhere out of sight, the sun having dipped just below the horizon. She turned to Silverstein, and shivered.

"I'm scared."

"Me too."

Silverstein took her hand and placed it on her chest, placing his own over her heart. He took a breath, and nodded to her. Bluish bio-electric lightning jumped between the two of them, arcing down into the surf around their feet, knocking them apart into the water. They both came up sputtering and coughing, latching onto each other as they did.

"Oh, hey there," Silverstein said, seeing a woman in her late twenties, hair cut short, looking like she'd fallen off a ship, maybe.

"Where are we?" Cerise asked, seeing a man about her age, in a button up shirt, and tattered dress slacks.

Silverstein laughed, squinting in the dark and looking around. "I have no idea. I'm really turned around."

Cerise giggled, letting go of him. "Oh, my God, so am I."

"Let's get out of the water, and try to figure out where we are," he said, offering her his hand.

She took his hand, and nodded. "All right."

THE END - BOOK 9

www.ingramcontent.com/pod-product-compliance
Lightning Source LLC
Chambersburg PA
CBHW070005260626

47159CB00005B/1677